CAGED

STAR BREED: BOOK THREE

ELIN WYN

ZAYDA

*R*ed, green, blue. Red, green, blue. The tags for the meds in the inventory flowed by in a sea of color, the only bright spots in the gray, dingy clinic.

Red, green, blue.

I'd done this yesterday, and would do it again tomorrow, since it counted as a useful task for the satellite. The mindless repetition let my thoughts fly free, as for the eighth time that morning I tried to figure out how to get a message to my handler.

"Take a break, Zayda," Denon called from the other corner of the prison clinic. "You're always working too hard."

Nominally assigned as the clinic medic, Denon didn't seem to worry at all about staying busy and useful. I glanced at my cuff. Still bright steady green. Good.

Maybe the time we spent patching up idiots who got into fights, or growers who ended up on the wrong end of equipment, earned him enough points to coast through.

I'd only been here for two weeks. Not long enough to have it figured out. I was waiting for a sign, some indication of which way to jump.

But nothing yet.

Red, green, blue.

"Come on, Zayda." Denon had sidled up next to me. I hadn't noticed his approach. Being trapped here was getting to me, wearing down my sharp edges.

His arm rested around my waist, making my skin crawl, but I kept a careful smile on my face. Until I knew who to trust and how I was getting out of here, I couldn't lose the clinic as a safe place.

Training made it easier to put up with a lot. But even I have limits.

I started to make another excuse but was saved by the opening of the clinic doors. Jado and Seig, hauling a third man between them.

As co-captains of the Skulls, the satellite's largest gang, they had sent plenty of people to the clinic, sometimes their own members.

But then I got a better look at the man they'd brought in with them.

Jado and Seig were big. This guy was bigger, even slumped unconscious, his arms stretched over their shoulders, legs and feet pulling behind as they dragged him through the door.

"Cuffs told us to bring this dude in," Jado said. "Too messed up to even get off the shuttle on his own power."

I raised an eyebrow. The shuttle that brought prisoners up to the satellite was programmed to stop recycling air as soon as the airlock doors opened.

Prisoners had two minutes to disembark. Occasionally someone would insist on trying to stay aboard for the return trip back to the station.

It never ended well.

By the end of those two minutes, they were usually convinced to try their chances on the satellite.

Denon sighed in exasperation. "Put him on one of the cots

until he comes out of it. Doesn't look like he's bleeding. Not much for me to do."

I slid out from under his arm. "I'll do a quick scan on him, just in case."

Denon turned away as I tapped my cuff. "May as well keep the meter filled."

From across the room the guy was big. Standing next to his cot, he was massive. Muscles bulged from his arms and chest, his shoulders too wide to be fully supported by the narrow cot.

There was no way he would fit into our antiquated full-body scanner, and I didn't even know if it was running today. I grabbed one of the handhelds and started at his feet.

The readings for - Oh. That was interesting.

I kept my eyes on the scanner and my mouth shut. But my mind spun frantically.

Jado and Seig were bullshitting with Denon. No one paid attention, no one cared.

In a career working for the Imperial spymaster, you hear a lot of rumors. The vast majority are lies, speculation, or, on a good day, somebody's drug-filled hallucinations laid on top of something they just watched on the triD.

I kept moving the scanner up his body, around his torso.

This guy was in good shape, in too good shape. The basic equipment we had here wasn't going to give me any details, but I could fill in the blanks myself. Someone had been doing more than just a little genetic editing. This was full-out manipulation, possibly even hybridization.

I hesitated for just a minute before starting the scan on his neck and head.

It would've taken a lot to knock out a man this healthy. I really didn't want to see the permanent damage that might have been done.

But I also really didn't want to hand the scanner over to

Denon. He might only be a half-trained medic, but even he would notice something odd in these readings.

The patient's hair was buzzed on the sides, a little long on top, with a few days' worth of scruff. His ears came to a slight point, barely noticeable if you weren't looking. With what I knew, I definitely was.

To my relief, all of his neural patterns read within normal ranges.

His head fell to the side and I fought back a gasp. A round mark with three prongs extending from the circumference, no bigger than my thumb, reddened the skin on the side of his neck. Carefully, I moved his head the other way, knowing already what I'd find.

No question about it, he'd been wiped.

His eyes flickered behind closed lids and his breathing sped up, just a fraction. Before I could move, a strong hand encircled my arm, just over the cuff.

Steady golden eyes met mine. "Who are you and what am I doing here?" The low growl of his voice wound around me as surely as his fingers.

"You're on Minor." It probably wouldn't mean anything to him. "I don't know who you pissed off, but it doesn't matter now."

No sign of recognition of the name, no sign of understanding of any kind. On impulse, I smoothed his hair back from his forehead and his eyes drifted closed.

If he was lucky, he'd dream of freedom, of being anywhere but here. I turned away, back into the nightmare.

MACK

*N*othing existed but fire and pain.

And then she appeared. Tiny, with golden skin and long black hair. Shadows in her eyes, her hands cool and soothing.

The fire reclaimed me, burning her away, leaving me nothing again.

I woke to the sound of her voice, and pushed myself up on one elbow to look around. A long box of a room, locked cabinets on the far side, where she stood, singing quietly to herself as she sorted through containers. A single deskcomm with a cracked screen in the middle of the long wall. Three other beds that looked as hard and narrow as the one I'd been lying on.

One door. No one else in the room.

I must've made a noise moving, because she whirled around, braid flying, expression wary.

I didn't move again, just nodded slowly in greeting.

With careful movements, eyes fixed on me, she tapped the panel in the wall and the sink slid out.

Gratefully, I drank the glass of murky water she handed me.

"Transport can be a little rough," she mentioned but her eyes wouldn't meet mine.

Transport? I didn't remember going on a trip. Darkness, I couldn't remember anything about where I'd been. "Where is this?" I croaked.

She smiled, "I told you before. You're on Minor."

I didn't recall asking before, and Minor sure didn't mean anything to me. She took the glass away and nestled it into a sterilizer for reuse.

"You're going to have to give me a little more than that, I'm afraid, darlin.'" I quickly stretched muscles in sequence. Other than some residual tightness and an itch on my left arm, everything seemed more or less in place.

She turned back, eyebrow cocked. "I am most certainly not your darlin.'" She stressed the word. "But I'll clue you in as to the rest of the set-up, since someone seems to have bumped you on the back of the head."

Her eyes flicked away, just for a moment. And just that fast I knew she was lying. Maybe not about everything, but something.

"Minor is the correctional facility satellite in orbit around Orem-5 Station. Since Orem-5 is one of the stations furthest into the Fringe, they've quit relying on Imperial security."

I shook my head. "This means nothing to me. Sorry." I scratched my arm again and then stared down at it. "And what the hell is this?

A broad silver cuff wrapped around my wrist, almost as wide as my hand, a stripe of glowing green on the outer edge.

I glanced over. The woman wore a matching one, but on her it almost covered her entire forearm. She sighed and rolled over a chair.

"That's your cuff, to make sure you behave. You've been sent here for some infraction of the rules back on the station." She shrugged, warding off my confused protests. "I know you don't remember. The station that we're in orbit around is Orem Station.

And people that do bad things on Orem Station get sent out here to be useful to society," she swept a hand in front of her, like brushing dust away, "until they're not."

"But what does this have to do with that?" I pried at the edge of the metal cuff, twisting and pulling until I received a sharp shock. I glared at her. "You could've warned me."

"You would've done it anyway. Everybody does." She tapped the metal with a fingernail. "Magnetic Access Control devices. We just call them cuffs. Behave, do enough useful activities for the satellite, get points. Do nothing, cause trouble, your points drop fast. You'll know about where you are by this." She raised her arm to display the bar of solid green that ran around the edge metal. "Try to stay in the green."

"What happens if I don't?"

"Lower your points enough, the mealpak dispensers don't work. You'll be shut out of the sleeping quarters. And become fair game for anyone else. There're a lot of people up here for a good reason. If they keep their own points high enough, they don't mind enforcing a little discipline on anybody who slips. Don't let it slide into the yellow."

"What's below yellow?" I asked.

She closed her eyes. "I don't know, but it can't be good."

"Well, then," I swung my legs to the side of the cot and started to push myself up but she held me back with one hand.

"Be damn sure you're ready to stand before you do. There's no way I can get you off the floor if you go down."

An unsettling thought crossed my mind. "This is a prison satellite and we're both prisoners, and there doesn't seem to be much in the way of guards roaming around."

"Self-enforcing rules, remote operation. Theoretically better than a panopticon."

I ignored the extraneous word, focused on my rising anger. "Do you know what I'm here for, what I've done?"

"Prisoner files are sealed from other prisoners. If no one

7

knows details about anyone's past transgressions, maybe people won't make the same mistakes." She grimaced. "I haven't really seen it work out that way."

"I could have been violent, could've been anything, and they left you alone with me?" I didn't even know who 'they' were, but they were on my shit list.

She looked amused. "Get too far out of line against another green, and the cuffs take you down. The jolt you got before was just a little love tap. The cuffs connect directly into the nerves of your arm." She stood up, pushed the chair away. "I told Denon I'd stay until you woke, but I'm about ready to call it a night. If you really are ready to go, let's see if we can find you quarters."

As I rose from the cot, my stomach rumbled. "I'd rather you showed me where to get one of those mealpaks you mentioned." I followed her out the door. "Not sure when I ate last."

She nodded and turned down the corridor. "Easy enough. I'm ready to head to the mess myself."

We walked in silence for a minute, and I tried to get my bearings. Why the hell was I on a prison satellite, in orbit around a station I'd never heard of? Actually -

"Hey, Zayda!" A blonde woman passing the other way called out, giving a small wave to my companion. "Running late?"

The woman, Zayda, tilted her head towards me, and the blonde's eyes grew big. "Just showing a new guy around."

The blonde bit her lips, gaze flicking between us until Zayda gave her a smile. "It's all good. I'll catch you later."

Her friend didn't look convinced, but continued on her way.

"Well, that was different," I muttered.

"What do you expect?" Zayda sounded more weary than angry. "She doesn't know you. I don't know you. The unknown is seldom a good thing around here."

"That's easy enough to fix". I stopped and held my hand out. "Hi, Zayda, it's nice to meet you. Thanks for being my tour guide. I'm -"

8

Only emptiness met me. A flash of pity crossed Zayda's face, but she took my hand anyway. "Must have been some bump on the head."

I pulled back, took the panic that threatened to overtake me, and pushed it down, shoved it into a box, and locked it.

"How can I not know my name?" I whispered.

"Does it matter?"

My head snapped back up. "Of course it does!"

"Would it change anything?"

I stopped the words that flew to my tongue. She was right. At this moment, whatever had happened to me didn't matter. Figuring out how this place worked, and then getting the hell out took priority. And then... I smoldered.

"Still need something to call you." Her voice summoned me from my thoughts.

I scratched at the edge of the cuff. "What the hell. Let's go with 'Mack'."

"Really?" Her eyes sparkled with humor, and her lips almost turned into a smile. "You're going to name yourself after the cuff?"

"Got anything better?"

"Nope."

"Tell me when you do, and we'll vote on it."

ZAYDA

For a guy who woke up in prison with no memory, Mack was decidedly smarter than I expected.

He watched the swirl of movement in the mess as we choked down our meal packs, the parade from pack dispenser to table to the racks of trays, absorbing it all.

He didn't ask a lot of stupid questions while we were eating, which was nice. In the two weeks I'd been here, I hadn't really felt the need for eloquent table conversation. Plenty to think about to fill the silence.

"No recycler?" He asked as we stood up to join the line towards the racks.

I shook my head. "Takes too much energy. Cheaper to have inmates use the sterilizer system than waste power to break it down and rebuild it as needed."

He frowned. "That seems inefficient. Don't tell me your star's gone dark."

"Nope, plenty of juice floating around out there. But anything we catch gets used on the farm, or sent down to the station."

"Farm." He repeated the word so flatly, I nodded to assure him I wasn't joking.

We inched our way towards the front of the line. The evening mess was winding down, and people would be heading out for the hour or so of recreation before curfew struck.

I was looking forward to just getting back to my bunk, but apparently that wasn't on today's list.

"Unless you've got special skills you suddenly remember, the farm is probably where you'll end up finding a job. They-"

"Hey, sweet cheeks." The slimy voice told me who'd sauntered up behind me.

I didn't bother to turn around, and there wasn't a way to keep him from moving. Larko, dark hair slicked back over his weasel face, leered before me. "Who's your new friend?" he asked, but his tone was anything but polite.

I didn't bother answering. There wasn't an answer that would make him go away. The only thing to do with scum like Larko and his little clique was ignore and avoid.

He took a step towards me and suddenly a solid wall of chest stood between us, Mack's bulk completely blocking Larko from my line of sight.

"Tell me more about this farm and its power needs. It sounds fascinating."

I couldn't help but grin, matching his own. "We've got the light of three suns, faint, but strong enough to power a good percentage of the station."

I tried to keep my voice neutral, even though the sight of Mack shifting to continue blocking Larko had turned into a surreal, amusing dance.

We reached the front of the line, turned in our trays to the inmates who had taken this particular task as their own, and headed out.

Larko and his friends were nowhere to be seen, thankfully.

"Who was that idiot, anyway?"

I gritted my teeth. "Someone I used to know, when I was a kid back on one of the Cilurnum stations. I had a chance to change my life. He didn't. Not surprised he ended up here." And I really didn't want to talk about this anymore. "Come on, I'll show you where the men's barracks are."

"Keeping genders separated seems like a lot of effort for a system that seems to rely on self-policing," Mack commented.

"Keeps down trouble. And, honestly, a lot of the women like it that way."

He nodded. "What happens if you aren't in by curfew?"

"The doors to the dormitories are sealed until the next cycle. If you're with a large enough gang, it's not a big deal. On your own, things might be a little dicey."

He stood at the door, frowning. "If I'm in here, who's going to see you safely back to the women's dorm?"

I laid my hand on his shoulder. "That's very sweet, but I'll be fine." He didn't look convinced. "We're nowhere near curfew. I'll be heading right back to the dorm and there're plenty of people around."

He still didn't look happy, but, honestly, I didn't need him to take care of me. Didn't want to have to try to figure out how much I could trust him. I showed him how to wave his cuff towards the sensor, then the door slid open and I stepped back.

"Good luck, I'm sure I'll see you around."

With obvious reluctance, he stepped through. The door immediately slid closed behind him, resetting for the next inmate.

Odd guy. I headed back to the other side of Minor, nodding to people I knew as I passed.

Most of them seemed to be here on fairly minor infractions. Nice enough folks, I was sure. I figured they'd do their time, get sent back home whenever their term was up, and only remember this place in odd moments, warn their kids to play it straight.

There were some bigger bruisers to be certain, like Jado and Seig, and treacherous thugs like Larko. For the good of the station, I hope the system kept them up here.

Mack, I couldn't figure out what he could have done. Big

enough, certainly strong enough, to have gotten into all sorts of trouble.

But he seemed like a genuinely nice guy. I remembered the wipe marks on the back of his neck and shuddered.

The only time I knew about people being wiped was after interrogation. Which meant my nice guy had to be mixed up in something pretty serious.

I headed back to the women's side, avoiding the sound of couples taking advantage of the time before curfew.

There might be curfew to ensure a functioning workforce, but some people didn't care.

I waved my arm at the scanner, looking forward to a quiet evening. Who knew, maybe tomorrow I'd look up Mack from the clinic's comms, see if I could find a little more information about him.

Inmate files were sealed, but that didn't mean everything on Minor was. And where there was one authorized way to open a system, there were always others. Just took a little looking.

The door scanner remained blank.

"Not again, this glitchy thing," I muttered.

I waved my arm, slower this time and then pulled it back to examine the cuff better.

My band had gone black.

I tapped it gently, then with a little more force.

Black. I'd never seen, never even heard of anyone's cuff going black.

"Door stuck again?" Ardelle's giggle would've gotten on my nerves once upon a time, but she was a genuinely kind woman. I couldn't imagine what had gotten her sent up here and, in all of our late-night chats, had never asked.

Her blonde hair was more than a little mussed, and the front seal on her jump suit askew.

"How is Jado doing," I asked, evilly amused to see her blush.

But she surprised me. "I don't want to talk about Jado, silly. I want all the details on that guy you were with earlier. Come on, get in so I can make you spill."

"I can't." I showed her my cuff and her face fell.

She gnawed her lip. "When did that happen?" she asked worriedly.

"I don't know. It was green at dinner. Must be some sort of malfunction." We both stared at the band, willing it to go back to a nice safe green.

She threw her shoulders back. "Come on in with me."

"You know that won't work. We'd just both get shocked, and lose points."

"You don't know that. If yours is malfunctioning it shouldn't shock you. Maybe it won't even realize the two of us are entering at once."

I shook my head, stepped back from her. "It's not worth the risk. Besides," I grinned, fighting for equilibrium, "how would I ever explain to Jado if I got his girlfriend hurt?"

"But what are you going to do?" she whispered.

"It's all right. I've got a plan."

She put her hands on her hips. "I've never even heard of a cuff malfunctioning and you've already got a plan for this?"

It was hard to explain that the vast majority of my previous life had required coming up with a plan for everything, no matter how small the chance. You never knew when one of those low probability contingencies could end up saving your hide.

All I said was, "You never know what can happen, right?"

I headed back into the corridor and waved as I turned the corner. "I'll see you in the morning."

"You better," she called, but I heard the whoosh of the door seal behind her before I took off.

I headed back to a spot two levels down, near the edge of the maintenance zone. I'd noticed it and unconsciously filed it away while stumbling around the satellite my first day here, trying to get my feet under me.

For all my talk of always being prepared, I certainly hadn't been ready for my cuff to go black.

I'D BEEN on my way back from securing a hiding place for the datachip. Maybe I'd been smug, overconfident. I'd spent almost 6 months on this assignment, most of it deep undercover in the warren of neighborhoods of the Orem station. Each strand of data had been carefully pulled, then teased out of a nest of rumor and innuendo.

Rumors had been checked, deleted files recovered. I'd already sent a comm to my handler, Stanton Grene, that I was ready to be brought in.

The stakes were too high to leave the disc on me. Life on a station at the Fringe of the Empire was always dangerous. Even if no one ever knew who I was, it wasn't impossible to fall off a glide between station levels or get hit too hard in a casual mugging.

I checked my chrono. Before long, I'd be back to the little apartment I'd made my own.

But I never made it.

When I woke up, I was in the clinic on Minor, Denon running a healing wand over the gash on my temple.

LOST IN MEMORY, I didn't hear them until it was too late.

Larko and one of his meat-headed goons blocked the next intersection.

I glanced around. No one was around, either everyone had gone in for curfew early or, more likely, the word had gone out that if people didn't want trouble they'd stay away.

"Looks like getting out of the lower levels didn't do you any favors, Zayda" Larko mocked. "We ended up in the same place after all." His smile spread across his face, but his eyes were flat and cold. "And what a shame. Somebody's been a bad girl. No points at all?"

His friend laughed and I rolled to the balls of my feet, ready to fight or dodge.

Another of their gang came around the corner behind me, boxing me in. I glanced up, but the ceiling tiles in this part of the satellite were fused. Annoyingly good work.

Larko stepped forwards as I crouched into a fighting position. "Such a shame. No points, no handy friend." He ran his eyes over me slowly, no doubt undressing me in what passed for his mind.

I might've been unsettled by it, but anger was more useful.

"Maybe you need some new friends? You should think about it."

Another step, then another, intent clear in every motion

There wasn't any point in wasting time or energy trying to talk my way of out this. No one would listen, they weren't reasonable sorts of guys. I stretched my shoulders, flexed the muscles in my arms. And looked the group of them over, weighing, appraising.

No way out but through, Stanton often said.

"Bring it," I muttered, and braced myself for the fight.

MACK

I walked through the door into chaos packed into a large, low-ceilinged room. Probably not a surprise that throwing a couple of hundred men into shared living quarters with minimal supervision is going to lead to a lot of mess.

I wrinkled my nose. Void, everyone here needed a shower. Maybe two.

Men milled back and forth, mostly with the casual bullshitting and nods of people who've agreed to leave each other alone.

Three men tangled in a scuffle in the far corner but no one seemed concerned.

I took a step towards them when a skinny older man with red rimmed eyes stepped in front of me.

"You're new here, I get that, I do, but I really would leave them alone if I were you." His squeaky voice rode up and down the scale with each word.

"And that would be why?" I asked, somewhere between confused and annoyed.

"It's the Monts, they all are, it's what they do. Either over a woman, or rations, or who's going to be in charge today, or tomorrow. Or yesterday," he giggled.

I stared at the combatants, noting their relative sizes, weights, fighting ability. They all seemed fairly evenly matched. I shrugged and turned away.

"Good idea, good idea," the skinny man half skipped next to me, patting my arm.

I looked down at him, frowning. "Who are you, and why do you care?"

"I'm Gozer, I am. I know everybody and everything in here. I keep my points up, yes I do, yes I do."

His hand trembled, just a bit. I wondered what he had been on when he was scooped and brought up here. But if he had information about the prison, maybe he could help me figure out what I was doing here.

But, first things first. "If you know everything about this place, how do I get a bunk?"

"Follow me, follow me." He patted my arm again and then, with his odd half-skip walk, darted in front of me, across the open room. A corridor led from the far wall with four more doors branching off of it, but he kept going to the end.

"Richo didn't come back yesterday, or the day before or before that. Nobody's claimed his bunk yet, it's in the back, nobody wants it." He looked up with a flash of embarrassment for a minute. "Most people don't want to be that close to me. Richo didn't mind, but he's gone now."

"If it's flat and nothing's crawling in it, you've got a deal. I've slept in worse."

The words jabbed at me. How did I know that? There was no memory to back up my claim, just a brief glimpse of hard-packed dirt under a vast, open night sky.

Oblivious, he bounced over to a small door at the end of the hall. I stooped to follow him into a narrow, barren room. The few beds were occupied by men that could all have been clones of Gozer: skinny, used up, fearful.

Gozer stood next to the sole unoccupied bunk in the back, stroking the thin blanket nervously.

"I do my shift in the laundry, I do, I do." He looked up slyly. "Our things get done first. Nice and clean."

The other men looked away, two resuming their conversation, the third flipping idly through a tablet.

I called over to him and he flinched. "Hey, you got access on that?"

"It's in dummy mode." He wrapped his thin arms around it, waiting for me to try to take the tablet from him. "Stuff comes in, but I can't get to the outer network."

That's what they tell you, I thought, but... a sharp pain bloomed in my temple where the headache that had hovered just out of sight since I woke in the infirmary took hold.

Gozer still stood anxiously by the bed, rocking from side to side.

"Looks great, thanks."

I sat on the edge of the bed. The thin mattress was possibly better than just lying on the permasteel deck, but just barely.

"Do you want Richo's job, too?" Gozer asked. "Nobody's seen him, and they liked him down on the farm. He was strong." He looked at me appraisingly. "You look strong, too."

I matched his smile. "I suspect I'd manage."

For all of his little twitches, Gozer obviously had some brains. Find a quiet place, find a big guy as protector, find a job. He had prison life figured out.

"What happened to Richo, anyway?" I asked.

Gozer's face fell. "Nobody's seen him. Must have got shipped out."

"That's a good thing, right? He's probably somewhere back on the station, waiting for you to get released so he can buy you a drink."

Gozer shook his head. "I don't think so, I don't think so."

What an odd little man. I leaned back on the bed, eyes closed.

One thing was right at least, the sheets were softened from repeated washings, and clean.

Tomorrow I'd ask him to show me how to get a job at this farm. Have to do something to keep my points up until I figured out what the hell I was doing here and how the hell I was getting out.

I thought about the sick system Zayda had described. Prisoners ruling other prisoners. Sure, it might work if you had some sort of innate belief in people. But I didn't.

I mentally walked back through the day, waking up in the clinic, and then...

There was nothing. It was like staring into a dark fog trying to conjure faces from the twisting mist.

And if I didn't have my memory, I had no idea what I had done to end up here. Had I robbed someone? Killed someone?

With the same sort of flash I'd had of that unknown night sky, I realized that yes, I had killed someone in the unknown past. But it wasn't something I felt guilt over, just flat. It was a job.

Suddenly the men's section with its noise and stench was too close, too confining.

"I've got to get out of here," I muttered.

"We all say that," Gozer giggled, and bounced on his bunk.

"No, right now."

He shot up with alarm. "You can't do that. Curfew is soon."

"Are the doors locked?"

"No, not yet. There's a warning siren. Don't get inside, have to stay outside. Outside with the ghosts." Gozer looked honestly worried.

"I'll be fine". My words, an echo of Zayda's earlier, didn't seem to calm him much.

I looked for anything to leave as a token that the bunk was spoken for, but all I wore was the light gray pants, shirt, and jacket I'd woken up in. No pockets. Wouldn't have been anything in them anyway.

"Keep my bunk for me, alright?"

He nodded, face still screwed up with concern. I headed back down the corridor, planning to go straight through the large gathering room to the halls of the corridor proper. There had to be one corner in this entire place quiet enough to think.

A large hand fell on my shoulder and I brushed it off. "Later," I growled, glancing back to see a pair of men who looked vaguely familiar. A tall blond and a stocky gray haired man to his side, both looking like they could handle themselves. On the neck of the gray haired guy I could see a black mark, disappearing into the collar of his jacket.

"You don't want to try to go this alone," the taller one said. "Loners tend to disappear." He turned away. "Let us know when you figure it out."

As the door slid shut behind me, I realized I didn't have any idea of the layout of the prison. I'd been to the clinic, the mess, and here.

"Let's change that," I muttered to myself as I jogged down a random hall. "Time for a scouting mission."

As I moved, I traced a map of the corridors in my head. Just having a better idea of the lay of the land eased some of the tension from my shoulders. One more pair of turns, and I'd head back to the dorm. No reason to take stupid risks on the first night.

Turning another corner, I heard the unmistakable sounds of a fight. I slowed, considered if I should get involved, then one sound cleared any doubt.

"Like hell, asshole."

That was Zayda's voice.

I tore through the corridors at full speed.

So focused on reaching her, I almost tripped over the arm of a guy sprawled across the corridor floor.

Zayda faced off against the jerk who harassed her in the mess hall. Another man sat slumped against the wall, shaking his head slowly.

The guy I had almost tripped on started to sit up. "Not today, bastard." I slammed his head back against the decking and he stayed down.

Zayda landed a sharp elbow into the asshole's throat and he staggered back, eyes wide with shock.

She crouched, sweeping her leg in front of her and knocking him to the floor. In a flash, she was over him, her knees hitting him in the shoulder socket while she choked him into submission.

Her fire, her fierceness mesmerized me. So much so, I almost didn't notice when the third joker pushed himself away from the wall.

"Back off, you bitch," he shouted and reached for her.

I reached him first and threw him back down the corridor. He hit the deck with a satisfying thud.

I turned back to Zayda. The idiot had finally gone limp.

"Nice job," I said as she stood up from him.

She whirled, fists ready to fly.

I raised my hands up. "Just me. Glad to see you didn't need help."

She looked at the guys on the deck past me. "Not much. Thanks."

Her shoulders slumped and with an unexpected flash of rage I saw a bruise beginning to bloom on her cheek. She saw where my eyes landed and scrubbed at it as if it were a stain she could just wash away.

"A couple of them landed. Shouldn't have happened. Got sloppy. As for why I'm still out here..." She raised her cuff and tapped it.

"I thought you said they didn't go below yellow."

"I said I'd never seen anybody below yellow. Probably just a malfunction, next dayshift I'll see what I can do. But for now..."

She looked tired, lost. I turned away, looked anywhere else. This felt too private, too personal. But still, something had to be done.

"I was thinking about getting my bearings, checking out some more of the satellite. I did sleep most of the day, and, to be honest, the men's quarters are a little...close."

Her smile only twisted half her face up, but I'd take it. "I've always wondered about that, but never enough to check it out."

She leaned against the wall, obviously weighing options, finger tapping against her thigh. "I've been waiting for a sign. Maybe this is it. Hell, maybe you're it. Let's go."

With a final kick at the prone form of her vanquished opponent, she headed off through the corridors.

A small knot unwound from my gut as I followed her.

It was a good thing she'd agreed to let me stay with her.

I'd planned to, either way.

ZAYDA

a s I headed towards my hiding spot, I tried like crazy not to limp, not to press my hand to my throbbing temple in front of Mack.

I don't know why, I didn't know him, had nothing to prove.

But, for whatever reason, maybe my own stupid pride, I didn't want to admit that Larko and his friends had gotten in more than just a couple of hits. Mack didn't ask why they'd targeted me, the one small miracle of the night.

On the station and up here, I'd let my training lapse, trying to keep my cover. Lot of good it had done me. And now that lapse could have gotten me killed.

Two levels down, I found a pocket of the maintenance section that, due to some quirk of the original satellite plans, was still in an unsecured area.

"There," I pointed.

Mack's eyes followed mine to an air vent, half hidden behind a bank of machinery.

"This is where you show me how big the rest of the vent is, right?" he joked.

"Oh, Void." I looked at the breadth of his shoulders and then again at the size of the air shaft. There was no way he would fit in there. It'd take hours with a torch just to cut a space for him.

He stepped forward to brush a section of hair that had fallen out of the braid away from my face. His touch surprised me, almost hesitant.

"You're overthinking this," he rumbled. "How often do you think people find this place?"

"I don't think anyone comes down here. No reason to, really."

"Let's get you settled, and I'll just hang out here to keep you company. How does that sound?"

It sounded easier than it should have. I felt worse when Mack took it on himself to move the machinery that blocked half the vent.

"Do you have tools for that?" he asked looking at the bolts holding the cover in place.

"I try to be prepared. Some days it works better than others." I found the tool kit I'd stashed on previous scouting trips and quickly undid the bolts.

Now that the shaft lay open before me, it felt silly to shimmy in. We were safe here. I was safe, wasn't I?

"I don't suppose you tucked a healing wand around here, too?" Mack's question interrupted the circles in my head.

"Nope. Didn't plan for that." I spun the wrench in my hands, then blurted on. "Look, I don't want you to think I don't trust you, but…"

He held up a hand. "You don't know me. Darkness, I don't know me. Get in there, and we'll make more plans later."

"I'll hold you to that." I slithered into the shaft. "I like plans. And lists." Not exactly comfortable, but having solid permasteel all around did wonders for my sense of safety.

"Horrors," he mocked, sliding down to lean against the opposite wall of the maintenance closet. "Not lists."

I crossed my arms in front of me and studied him. His eyes were closed, but he didn't seem headed towards sleep. Technically, even if he couldn't get into the shaft himself, he could reach in, drag me out.

"I can hear you thinking from over here." He cracked an eye. "Are you sure you don't want me to leave?"

I sighed. "No." I propped my chin in my hands, too tired and sore to hold my head up. "Ever since I was brought here, I can't stop thinking about ways I could be attacked. I shouldn't have let myself be taken."

He tilted his head, and, just like in the infirmary, I was caught by his tawny eyes. "How bad manners is it for me to ask what you were arrested for?"

"I wasn't."

"What? Then why are you here?"

"Because someone wanted something I had. I've been trying to decide what to do next."

"Isn't there some sort of appeals board, something?"

"That's not going to help me. I know why I'm here, but I don't know who's behind it."

"Well, you're one up on me, then." He scrubbed his hands through his hair. "I keep feeling like I need to get somewhere, but, every time I reach for it, it's a blank. If I'm your sign, I'm a pretty crappy one."

I grinned. "We'll manage."

"What are you going to do about your cuff?"

"I don't know." Options scrolled through my mind, each demanding to be balanced, analyzed. "I need to be able to access the rest of Minor. There's got to be a protocol for when this happens. I'll ask Denon at the clinic tomorrow." The need for a contingency plan gnawed at me. "If I can't get it working again, the only reason to keep it on would be to blend in, and you can see how well that went."

"Don't forget about our lovely dining experience." His eyes narrowed. "It sounds like you think keeping it on is optional."

Damn. That's what I get for thinking out loud.

"And now you're all wary again." He stretched out on the deck, rolled his broad back to me. "Sleep now. We'll figure it out in the morning."

I wanted to stay awake, figure out what I was going to do next, if I couldn't get the cuff reactivated. I've been waiting for a sign, maybe this really was it. I stared at Mack's back, listening to his breathing in the tiny room, until I drifted into sleep.

Without a chrono, it's damn hard to tell the time. Back on the station, most levels had lights rise and dim in time with an Imperial day cycle, just to try to keep things more or less in sync. It worked that way in the dorms, but in this forgotten little nook it was just the same mostly dark grayness.

I checked my cuff out of habit and then kicked myself. The status band was programmed to dim during the night cycle, but, obviously, that wasn't going to help me now.

So I had no idea how long I'd slept when I jolted awake.

I strained my ears but couldn't hear anything over the sound of my heart beating, couldn't figure out what had dragged me from sleep.

Then I heard it again. "Go to hell," came a soft murmur. And then a low grunt, like someone being hit.

In the dim light I could see Mack tossing and turning.

I shimmied halfway out from the air shaft, then paused. This wasn't any of my business. The half-light was enough to see the look of anguish on his sleeping face. Whatever he was remembering in his dreams, it had to be pretty awful.

I wiggled closer to him, laid my hand on his chest, half prepared to duck back in case he was one of those who woke up swinging. There'd been a guy like that in training.

"Mack, it's okay, wake up."

He flinched, and then relaxed under my hand. I could feel the muscles of his chest beneath the thin fabric of the prison-issued jacket. His breathing slowed, and, although he didn't wake, the lines of strain on his face eased.

Good enough.

I started to head back to my hidey hole, but his hand shot out and pulled me to him, tucking me against his side.

This wasn't what I had planned. His arm wrapped over my waist like a vice. Well, I thought as I pillowed my head on his shoulder, it wasn't any less comfortable than sleeping in the air shaft.

And I had a feeling that Mack was just as solid as permasteel walls.

MACK

"IT'S TIME TO GO."

*T*he command rang clearly in my ears, even as I jolted awake to a sitting position.

"Hey," Zayda fussed sleepily. "Quit moving."

Sometime during the night she had come out from the safety of her air vent to sleep curled against my side. I shook my head. It seemed so out of character for her. Then I remembered a cool touch in the middle of dreams of fire.

Maybe I just didn't know her well enough to know what was really in character at all.

The stripe on my cuff still glowed green, fractionally brighter than it had during the sleep. How long would it take to shade to yellow without restocking my points?

I reached down to where Zayda had curled up on herself and lightly touched her shoulder. "It's morning. Let's go see if we can get your cuff sorted."

Her eyes flew open as if she had only been resting, then I could almost see the list scroll in her mind, boxes ready to be checked.

"We should get you to the farm first." She sat up and began to rebraid her hair.

"Nothing doing." After the events of last night, I was going to see her safely to the clinic, no matter what she said. "You can give me directions from the clinic. Until you get that thing fixed, you need to stay with people you trust."

Zayda huffed, but didn't argue. Back onto the main level, she stopped suddenly. "There's no point in me going to the mess, but you've got to be hungry."

I shrugged. "I think my stomach would consider it a favor if I missed one of those meal packs. Besides, if I'm going to be on some sort of a farm, there's got to be snacks around, right?"

She turned, mouth set and grim. "Don't try to steal the product. Seriously. Having a source of fresh grown food is one of the things that's made Orem Station so rich. The only person I've heard of who tried swiping some for himself ended up losing points immediately, almost got beaten to death."

Her wide eyes held just a touch of fear.

"I promise, I'll keep my fingers out of the cookie jar," I joked.

"Cookie jar? What the hell is a cookie jar?"

I stopped, shook my head. "No idea." I had a flash, an image of an older woman, scolding me and...my brothers? Then it was gone again.

"Must've been something somebody told me when I was growing up. I don't remember now."

Zayda tucked her hand around the crook of my elbow and squeezed my arm. "Never mind, it's a perfectly reasonable phrase. I'll try to use it myself."

I used my cuff to trigger the doors into the clinic and Zayda slipped inside alone. I stuck my foot on the track to keep it from closing immediately.

She looked around briefly. "Denon's not in yet, no surprise. I can use his passcode to log into the comms, see if I can figure out what's wrong with my cuff."

I didn't like leaving her there, but she'd shown she was a competent fighter, and she had more than a small interest in her personal safety. So I fought down my instincts and forced a grin. "You have fun with that. I'll see if I can get a little hurt and come check on you during the day."

She smiled and returned, "You are an odd, odd man. But thank you."

The door slid closed behind me and I headed through the labyrinth of corridors down to the level called the farm.

Even though Zayda had told me the satellite raised enough food for the needs of the station below, as well as for export to this section of the Fringe, I was surprised at the complexity of the system before me.

It must take up an entire floor of the satellite, trays stacked in racks almost to the ceiling, soft light coming from beneath each tray to shine on the plants beneath. I could hear the faint sound of water, then noticed a network of tubes connecting each of the trays.

As I took it all in, a battered 'bot rolled down one of the pathways. Its screen was set for telepresence, but the image was grayed out, unrecognizable. If there had ever been anyone at the other end, it was more likely that now the 'bot had simply been programmed to greet and assign workers as efficiently as possible.

"New arrival?" a voice crackled from the speakers.

"Yep, someone told me to come down here and make myself useful."

"There's plenty to do." It rolled back the way it had come from. "Follow me."

As we went through the narrow paths between the racks, the 'bot recited the variety of tasks needed to keep the operation running.

"Should be self-sustaining, even down to the harvest, but machinery hasn't been updated in years. Nutrient lines get clogged, the compost mixer broke down too long ago to remember, and the rack loader works at about half capacity."

The 'bot rotated its top half towards me, continuing to roll on, it's blank screen giving me the eerie feeling of being sized up.

"You're too big to be of any use trailing the tubes, so loading and mixing compost it'll be."

Other men and women had started filtering in, taking up their tasks with little chatter. "Makes no difference to me, as long as I'm useful."

A noise escaped the 'bot, enough like a snort that I wondered how much latitude the AI it housed had been given.

"Helpful attitude from the beginning. We don't see much of that around here." It turned another corner, out from the rows of growing racks, into a more open, industrial- looking area. "Don't cause trouble. This is your life now."

I stopped. "'My life now'? I'm just up here like everyone else, for the terms of my sentence." Which I didn't remember, but I was pretty sure that that's how prison worked, right?

The 'bot didn't pause. "Who told you that? Once you're here, you stay. At least, you better hope you stay."

Well, that was going to put a crimp in my plans. I spent the morning stirring piles of compost with two other surly looking men. They weren't particularly forthcoming when I tried to make small talk, or even direct questions.

The job required that we stand waist deep in a vast metal half-cylinder, stirring and churning half-rotted remnants into sludge. We worked around the tines of the huge mechanical forks that still hung from beams overhead.

I looked at the broken cables leading through the machinery. "What are the chances those things start up while we're in here?" I asked.

The bald guy, whose name I still hadn't gotten, shrugged. "You move fast. Most of the time, the machinery stays dormant. Every now and then it seems to get a little kick, though." He grinned, not in a particularly friendly way. "Why do you think there was an opening on the unit?"

36

Well. That was reassuring. We stirred and turned and churned the stinking mass until the bell rang for a break.

The three of us climbed the ladder out of the vat and headed to rinsing tubes. As we pulled our uniforms back on, I noticed that both men had the same black mark below their ears as the man who had approached me in the men's dorm last night.

"What's that about?" I asked.

The bald guy crossed his arms. "Marks us as Skulls, man. I'm surprised Jado hasn't talked to you already. You're big enough, you'd be an asset."

I thought back. "Tall guy? Blond? He might've tried to last night, but I had stuff going on."

The other one, skinny with shifty eyes, finally spoke up. "You don't want to blow off Jado. The Skulls are the strongest gang up here, you can't go it alone."

I nodded, and then remembered what the 'bot had said earlier that morning. "But what about when you go back to the station? Do you want a mark like that where everyone can see that you did time?"

They both looked at me with something in between shock and amusement on their faces. "Man, the only way out of here is when the black ghosts come for you."

We stood in line with the others to get our mid-shift rations, my apparently stupid questions having finally done the trick to break the ice.

I had promised to get up to the clinic and Zayda, but this sounded like information we needed.

"Black ghosts," I continued after we got our trays. "Sounds like some sort of boogeyman, stories to keep us in line."

"No way." Now that he had an audience, the shifty looking one seemed more than happy to spread the story. "I've seen them, just the once, but it was enough. They only come at night, that's why curfew is such a big thing."

"The governor doesn't want anyone seeing those crazy fuckers." He shuddered, seemed genuinely rattled. "Wish I hadn't. Black uniforms, black gloves - and man, they don't have faces!"

Well, that wasn't going to be as helpful as I'd hoped. Apparently someone had found a way to stay hopped up even here. Maybe I should ask if he'd share his stash with Gozer.

ZAYDA

*T*he quiet of the clinic was oddly comforting. Since I'd been up on Minor, I'd probably spent more of my waking hours in this small room than anywhere else on station.

I logged into the deskcomm with Denon's credentials. He never bothered to change his password, seemed never to have heard of basic security.

Yet another reason I couldn't trust him.

"Cuff maintenance, it's gotta be here somewhere," I muttered to myself.

Surely this couldn't be the only case of a malfunctioning unit. Just because I'd never seen one didn't mean it never happened.

But, so far, I wasn't finding anything. Like all communications on the Minor, the terminal was locked down. Information could come in, but nothing could get out.

Even with full access, I wasn't sure where else I would look for a manual on the damn things without giving myself away completely.

I kept hunting until finally I found a subdirectory with a list of emergency reset and control frequencies.

I had always known I could get the cuff off, some variant of the device was used in a number of Imperial facilities, and they all had some of the same basic characteristics. Usually operations were controlled by a series of frequencies. Facilities could reset and customize theirs, but most didn't bother.

Despite myself, thoughts of Mack wormed through my focus. Why had he been sent up here?

A disturbing worry gnawed at the back of my mind. How would I know if he'd really been memory wiped? The marks - that could be a tattoo, easily recreated once you knew what the burn pattern looked like. I could search for his file, nothing was really sealed. But that wouldn't tell me anything other than his cover story.

What if it was just an act, a way for the governor to get close to me, discover where I'd hidden the disk? His scanner readings only confused things. He was obviously the product of genetic engineering, to a level illegal in the Empire. Did that make him more likely to be a tool of one of the Syndicates?

I didn't try to think of the details of my mission often. Safer to keep my mind as blank as possible, to not risk giving myself away.

But now I needed to examine the entire project. I knew I'd already been betrayed by at least one person. Did Mack fit into the pattern as another possible traitor?

When I arrived on Orem, it had taken a while to get past the rumors, find actual proof of the criminal activities by the station's governor. As governor, he had the ultimate authority on Minor - it had been the logical place for his goons to toss me for holding. It would be easy enough for him to plant another inmate, make it look like he needed help, in an effort to get close to me.

The criminal activity was clear, but I had stayed longer than I should have, trying to identify who the governor's partners were. There were plenty of little villains, but a majority of his business went through one far outpost - and I couldn't find any details on who ran it. If we rolled the governor up, I didn't want bigger fish getting away.

When his goons had grabbed me, they'd made a mistake. No one knew where I'd hidden that chip. And that meant they didn't know how much I'd uncovered.

I'd bet he'd do a lot to find that out. Even try to plant someone on the inside to get close to me.

And yet… I thought about Mack's troubled night.

I'd heard his breathing - he was sleeping, I was sure. The nightmare wasn't faked, but, in the cold artificial light of morning, I couldn't say that it was proof that he had been wiped.

Finally, I found the list of cuff controls and scanned it quickly. Just as I'd guessed, Minor hadn't bothered to switch from the factory presets. And there was what I needed to reset my cuff to green. Good enough.

As I started closing screens, a subdirectory caught my eye. I brought it to the foreground, and for a moment stopped breathing.

Transmission logs. Outgoing. And from this terminal.

I glanced at the door, Denon still hadn't come in. From his regular pattern I could expect several more minutes of privacy, but the urge for caution was stronger than ever.

Quickly, I flicked open the most recent of the messages. I could work my way back, but I needed to know what was going on now.

Whatever you did failed. Don't know why you thought the bitch would come back here. Told you plenty of times she wasn't warming up to me. Just come and get her. But I still earned my deal, right?

I froze. The 'bitch' seemed very likely to be me.

I checked the timestamp on the messaging. It was after curfew. Denon must've had a way to get out of the dorms and back here, to the single terminal with access to the outside world.

The message was clear between the lines. Something had been deliberately done to my cuff in the expectations I would come back to the clinic. But why?

It had to be about the chip. There was nothing else anyone would want.

But who had he told to come pick me up? Where would be worse than here?

My throat dry, my eyes flicked back and forth between the screen and the door. There had to be more in the logs.

I picked a previous message at random, no time to go through them methodically. From the time stamps, they looked like daily reports, stretching back to a few days before I had been kidnapped.

Bitch isn't warming up. I don't know. Maybe she just doesn't like guys. I still get my deal, right?

I stuck my tongue out. That sounded exactly like Denon. Obviously, if I wasn't into him, I wasn't into guys at all. Douche.

Time for one more. I picked one of the earliest messages.

I'm telling you, I want immunity from the ghosts, or no deal.

Ghosts?

My heart thudded in my chest as I checked the chrono. I didn't know what was going on, but it was too close to when Denon usually came strolling through the door to risk checking further. I swore under my breath. I could have sent a message to Stanton, let my handler know where I was being kept all along. But now I was out of time. Next time I wouldn't hesitate.

I closed all of the windows, went back into the system history and wiped my tracks, until the comm looked just as it had when I arrived. But I couldn't leave the thoughts of those messages alone.

Ghosts?

The word echoed in my head while I disassembled the hand-held scanner, used the calibration tool to reset the frequency.

That Denon had been co-opted to spy on me wasn't a surprise. If anything, it explained why he was always just a little too friendly, a little too accommodating about logging my tasks as useful, even though they were obviously busy work.

But ghosts? How do you get immunity from ghosts?

By the time Denon sauntered into the clinic, I'd returned the scanner to its regular condition, replaced it in the cabinet, and was busily making sure we had enough bandages and gauzes. It looked like we were well stocked into the next century.

Denon hesitated just an instant when he saw me. The flicker in his eyes was enough to confirm what I had read in the messages. Something was going on, and he was a part of it.

"Leave that for now," he said after a moment. "Just heard over the comms that the gasket blew on a poor sucker working the sterilizer in the mess hall. We'll need to get the hyperbaric gear prepped."

We didn't have a full hyperbaric chamber, of course. The best we could do was seal and wrap it one section at a time in something like a large pressurized envelope, and dope the victim up. Out of habit, I checked the slender oxy tanks. Something else we were well enough stocked with.

By the end of shift, I was exhausted. Friends of the burn victim had come and gone throughout the day, and one of them had enough sense to offer to bring us meal packs.

I'd turned her down. After seeing the steam-scalded flesh blister across the man's chest, I didn't have much of an appetite.

"Go ahead and call it a night," Denon said. "I'll keep an eye on them for a while." He'd been professional and courteous, but a bit remote, all day.

Maybe knowing I was due for someone to come and 'get' me made him want to put a little distance between us.

"Sure. I'll see you in the morning." He didn't look up from the comm screen.

Outside the clinic doors, I leaned against the wall. I didn't have all the information I wanted. Hell, I didn't have nearly enough to even make a reasonable guess at the right decision.

But I'd run out of time.

A large shape loomed out from the side corridor and I stiffened, ready for another fight.

43

"Just me," Mack's low voice rumbled. "You look like you had a hell of a day," his glance dropped to my cuff, "despite getting some maintenance taken care of."

"Void, yes," I sighed.

Time to choose, Zayda.

"Why don't you buy a girl a drink, and I'll tell you all about it."

He ran his hand through his brush of hair and gave a grin. "Think I could use one of those myself, darlin'. And I've got a few things to tell you, as well."

As we approached, you could hear the heavy bass music reverberating through the deck.

"What the hell is this?" His eyes bounced from couple to couple in the makeshift bar. Ramshackle booths had been jury-rigged out of spare parts, machinery, anything that people could get their hands on.

Curtains made of drop chutes partitioned off part of the large room, and it didn't take particularly good hearing to figure out what was going on behind the fabric, with the faint illusion of privacy.

"Anytime you put people somewhere, you know somebody's gonna figure out how to make a still. Welcome to the Down Low." I gestured expansively, and headed to the bar. "I'm warning you, it's terrible."

MACK

*M*y nostrils flared as I took in the room. Apparently once a series of store rooms, it stunk of sweat and sex and stimulants. I didn't like this. Too many people, too much noise. But if I wanted to tell Zayda what I'd found out, little though it was, it looked like I'd be doing it here.

I joined her at the length of battered permasteel that laid over a couple of crates, pretending to be a counter.

A woman with dark skin, her hair falling around her face in a cascade of short braids, was deep in conversation with Zayda.

"I'm telling you, girl," the bartender said. "You worked on saving my guy today. You're not paying for your drinks." She looked my way and I could feel her eyes trail up and down my chest. "And if this big boy's with you, I can stand him his first couple, too. Not sure if it will do much to him."

Zayda laughed. "No idea yet, but I guess we'll find out."

The woman brought back two scavenged glasses, half filled with a clear liquid. The acrid scent overwhelmed everything else in the room. That wasn't a bad thing.

"Come on, big boy," Zayda teased. "Let's see if we can find a space."

I sipped the drink as I followed her, noting the curve of her hip as she almost danced through the crowd to find a clear spot by a wall.

It burned all the way down. I took another sip as I joined her, our backs against the wall.

"Want to tell me what we're doing here, darlin'?"

She put her drink down, untasted. "Sorry. But I don't know anywhere else on Minor that we can talk without anyone noticing. No idea what phrases are set to trigger a deeper search, but I'll bet we might use one or two tonight."

"How much of it is wired?" I asked.

"No idea." She looked tired, but, beyond the exhaustion, I could see a fire in her eyes. "But if you were running the show, wouldn't you have ears everywhere you could?"

Likely, but that left even more questions unanswered. "Then why would they allow this sort of place to keep going? Certainly the cuffs could be set to not allow access, or give a shock every time a certain number of people gathered in a space outside of the mess or dorms."

"I don't know." She shook her head, frustrated. "There're too many things I don't know. I'd suspect as long as the station gets the power and their crops delivered on time, maybe the governor just doesn't care. Maybe someone on his staff realizes the people stuck in here need a pressure valve, some sort of release during their sentence."

I took another sip. It didn't get any better. "Makes sense. Especially since a sentence up here seems to be for life."

Her eyes flew open. "What do you mean?"

I told her what I'd found out – the black ghosts that terrified tough men, the one-way sentences, everything. "You've never asked anyone how long they were up here for?"

"No, it didn't seem like relevant information." She reached for her drink, set it down again. "That was stupid of me."

I turned to face her directly, blocking her view of the room.

46

"No, I just think you've had your mind on too many other things." I laid my hand over hers where it rested by her glass. "People keep telling me you can't go it alone here."

Her gaze fixed on my hand for a long moment, then she met my eyes with a faint smile. "Maybe I can't."

The commotion of the room behind us faded away as I leaned towards her. "Maybe you don't need-"

"Hey, sweet cheeks. Want to dance again?"

Zayda's jaw clenched, and I turned to see the idiot and his friends who had attacked her last night.

I slammed down the rest of my drink.

"Fuck. This. Nonsense."

I took a step towards him, Lardo, Largo, whatever the hell. It didn't matter, and was about to matter a hell of a lot less.

"Listen here, dirtscum," I growled, and the crowd around us stilled, as if sensing the dark attraction of impending violence. "If you don't stop harassing her, I will break you into so many pieces they won't be able to scrape you up off the deck."

The weasel threw his chin up, narrowed eyes still focused on Zayda. "Zayda and I go way back. Besides, you can't do anything to me." He tapped his cuff. "I'm full green. All stocked up. You try anything, and you'll-"

"Don't know, don't care," I rumbled, and decked the bastard, knocking him back into the crowd. The shock on my arm was annoying, but not exactly a deterrent.

"Sorry about that, folks." I turned to the idiots who'd been with the stack of human garbage. "Are you next?"

"No, no." He and his companion went and pulled their leader up off the floor. His head lolled to the side. I half-hoped I hadn't killed him, but, at the moment, I wasn't terribly concerned.

A light touch at the small of my back. I didn't even turn, I knew it was Zayda.

"How's your arm?" she muttered, too low for anyone else to hear.

"Not really a big deal, actually. I knew it was coming." I rubbed my arm above the cuff, the tingle already fading. "Totally worth it. Except now, I'm not sure how much of a conversation we're going to be able to have in private." I nodded to the watching, whispering crowd.

"Well," her hand slid up my back and I stiffened at the heat in her caress, "we can always pretend we're here for the same reason everyone else is. Once they're sure there's nothing more exciting coming, I expect they'll go back to their own business."

I turned back towards her, and Zayda stepped into my embrace as if she were a part of me. Her arms wrapped around my neck and I lifted her up, braced her back against the wall while her legs wrapped around my waist.

She rained tiny kisses up the side of my neck and I fought the urge to fist her hair, pull her head back, and plunder her mouth with my own.

"You're good at this," her breath tickled my ear and I shifted her weight to free one hand, sliding it up the rough fabric of her jacket, my fingers barely grazing the curve of her breast.

She panted and I took advantage of her distraction to nip at her earlobe. "So, what are we planning that can't be overheard?"

I nuzzled her neck, breathing deeply of her scent beneath the harsh industrial soap.

"What?" her eyelids fluttered and she pulled herself back together. "Right." She ran her nails lightly down the back of my neck and I pulled her tighter into my chest. "If the black ghosts, which we can assume are soldiers in some sort of uniform, come and take people away, never to be seen again, I don't think I want to go with them."

My workmate's description ran through my mind, and suddenly a clear picture formed, a looming figure dressed in black from head to toe, with no discernable head, just an opaque black dome.

"Ow!" Zayda jumped. "Careful!"

"Sorry," I muttered and forced my hands to unclench. "Just thought I remembered something, nothing good."

She broke away, laid her hand on my cheek. "But remembering at all has got to be a start, right?"

"Doesn't do us any good right now." Dread certainty uncoiled from my gut, set sharp knives against my spine. "Right now, we need to get off the satellite."

"Agreed." She tilted her head forward until it rested on my chest. "I've never heard of anyone escaping, but I'd bet if anyone knew about attempts, even failed ones, it would be the Skulls."

"Jado, great," I groaned. "I keep hearing I need to go talk to him."

"No time like the present," she said and, with a wiggle, shimmied out of my arms. Zayda reached back, interlacing her fingers with mine and tugged me towards the back of the room.

Passing through the fluttering walls, the brief flashes of skin, the sound of a woman's moans, and the aroma of arousal did nothing to help quench the burning need that Zayda's touch had ignited in me.

"Here we are," she said brightly and squeezed my hand before calling out. "Hey, Ardelle! Everybody decent?"

A happy laugh answered her, and then the curtain was pulled back to reveal what must have been the entire back section of one of the storerooms. It had been converted into an office or a sitting room of some kind. A few chairs purloined from the mess hall were scattered about, and a low bed was half-shielded by a paneled screen.

The dim lights covered most of the dinginess, and a few colorful scraps of fabric made a valiant effort to brighten the room.

Bouncing up and down in excitement was the same blonde woman who'd scowled at me last night.

She looked at the two of us and grinned, eyes filled with mischief.

"I was so worried when I didn't see you in the mess this morning!" She hugged Zayda, pulling us both into the room. "You could have come by the dorm or sent someone with a message to let me know that you made it through the night."

"I'm sorry." Zayda hugged her back. "Without my cuff working, I couldn't get into most places. And then, there were complications."

The blonde's eyebrows came together. "What kind of complications?" She stepped towards me, ready for a fight.

Zayda pushed her back. "Ardelle, stop. This is Mack. He helped with the complications and then made sure there weren't any more. He's one of the good guys."

"He better be." Hands still on hips, Ardelle didn't look particularly convinced.

I liked her. It was pretty obvious that I could've broken her in two, but Ardelle didn't seem to care as long as her friend was safe. That worked for me.

A form rose from the dark corner of the room and I stepped in front of Zayda without thinking.

"Took you long enough," Jado said, stepping from the shadows. "Ready to join up?"

He slipped an arm around Ardelle, who snuggled into him. "Never thought your friend was up for sharing, babe." He winked lewdly at Zayda, and my fists clenched.

Zayda's voice could have frozen the entire farm level. "I'm not."

Ardelle poked the gang leader in the side. "And neither am I, jerk."

He dropped a kiss on the top of her head and shrugged. "I know. But never hurts to double-check these things, right?"

"Anyway, what are you two looking for?" He waved towards the cluster of chairs, then sat himself, pulling Ardelle into his lap. "As much as I think you'd be an asset to the Skulls, you don't have the vibe of someone who's much of a joiner."

I nodded. "I appreciate it. I think," the memory was hazy, but the feeling was solid, "I already have a team."

"But that's not what we're here about," Zayda steered the conversation back with laser focus. "What do you know about previous attempts to get off Minor?"

"You can't," Ardelle breathed, face pale. "There's no way. And, if you try, they come…"

My jaw tightened. "Let me guess. The black ghosts?"

ZAYDA

$\mathscr{A}$rdelle nodded, looked from Mack to me. "I know it's not what you're used to, but you can make a decent life up here. Once you get the system figured, it's not that different from anywhere else." She bit her lip, pleaded with me to understand. "Home is where you make it, right?"

Void, I wished it could be that simple. Instead I reached for her hand. "You've been a good friend, and I'm glad you're happy, even here. But I have unfinished business back on Orem. And," I closed my eyes, leaning back in the chair, as if the weight of the station pushed me into the deck, "I'm pretty sure the ghosts are coming for me anyway. Soon."

"No!" Ardelle's denial was flat, unaccepting. "They can't. You haven't done anything!"

"It's alright, babe." Jado stroked her hair.

She spun in his lap, eyes full of fury. "How can you say that?"

"Because we're going to get her out of here. Just need to figure out how."

"Fine." She settled back down, but her stiff spine told me she'd been badly frightened.

"I'm sorry, Ardelle. I didn't mean to drag you into this. I just didn't know where else to turn for information."

"Silly. We're friends. What else would you do?"

"Alright," Jado said, eyes focused on nothing. "First issue is the cuffs. As long as you're wearing that, they'll know where you are anyway."

"Not really an issue." The relief to finally be telling someone, anyone, a small fragment of the truth eased some of the weight on my chest. "Tell you what. As payment for helping, I'll get you the codes to operate them, and the tools you'll need to use on them."

"See," Jado turned to Mack, who still didn't look entirely happy we were here. "Teamwork gets you everywhere."

"Next, transport. You don't want to go with the ghosts, which seems reasonable. But the only other ship that comes here is the rotation shuttle. Every three days, needed or not."

"That what I came up on?" Mack asked.

Jado looked between the two of us, startled. "You don't even remember getting on? They messed you up, man."

Ardelle filled Mack in. "It's pretty efficient, really. Drop off the prisoners, unload whatever supplies there are, then vent the atmosphere." She grimaced. "Not like there's ever much more than those damn meal packs. We could use some real maintenance. This place is gonna fall out of the sky sooner or later."

"When it's empty, me and the boys fill it back up with the harvest from the farm," Jado added. "Atmosphere gets turned off again, and it heads back down to the station. Entire thing's on automatic. Which means there's no one to bribe for the trip, pick up a passenger or two."

Mack frowned. "Don't the plants need oxygen for the trip back?"

Ardelle shook her head. "Nope, the farms are the reason the air quality is pretty decent up here. Our air scrubbers haven't been at full capacity since no one knows when." She swung a foot loosely in his direction. "Haven't spent much time around green things, have you?"

Mack glanced my way, rubbed his jaw. "Not until this morning, really."

"Plants take in CO2, put back out oxygen. But it wouldn't be enough to keep someone alive for the trip down, you know."

"How long is the trip, do you think?" In the time I'd been on Orem, I'd barely heard about Minor, never really thought about it.

"Our orbit isn't that far out," Jado answered. "The return trip likely takes under an hour. Once we figure out how to hide you from whoever's doing the unloading on the station, all you have to do is survive the trip without breathing."

Mack started to say something, and I had an instant of fear that he'd remembered something about his unusual biology. I didn't know all of his capabilities, and I hated hiding things from our new allies, but that was one wild card I wasn't ready to have out on the table yet.

I talked over him quickly. "I've got a plan for that, actually. It should work, but I might need a little help getting some things out of the clinic."

Jado cocked an eyebrow. "I'll trust you to look after your own breathing, then."

A pang of guilt struck me. "What about repercussions up here? If we escape, what are they going to do to anybody who helped us?"

Jado grinned, and I could see he'd already thought of a way to turn this to his advantage. "You'll need to leave your cuffs up here anyway, we can play a fine game of hide and seek. No reason for them to know you're off-station."

"Besides," Ardelle chimed in, "what are they gonna do? Stop feeding us? If we can take the cuffs off, why would we ever send another leaf or sprout down to them?" "

"I think we've just kicked off a rebellion," I said slowly. It was a crappy system, and, honestly, I was perfectly happy to be part of the end of it.

"You got it, honey," Jado winked. "And you're looking at the new king and queen of Minor."

Ardelle poked him. "Idiot," she muttered, but she didn't look that upset with him.

"What about the ghosts, whatever they really are? They come and go when they want," Mack added. "They've got to have some controls over Minor, or at least access to the landing bay. Who else does? The governor? Who on Orem can control the basic functions of the satellite? You've got to assume they've got some fail safes and booby traps in place."

Jado tapped his fingers on the arm of his chair, eyes narrowed, planning. "Couple years ago, we brought in a genius geek to the Skulls. No fighter, and a crappy attitude, but I figured she'd be a useful investment someday. Her cuff is super restricted access, she's never been in anywhere near the primary systems of this place. Once she's able to do anything she needs, go anywhere with the right overrides? I'm betting she can make this place a fortress."

"It's your people," Mack looked at Ardelle, and we both knew what he was thinking. Jado would be risking everyone on the bet that his genius could control the satellite faster than whoever was trying to take it back from Orem. "Your bet."

"She can do it," Ardelle said with a tone of finality. "Besides, if there really is a chance we can get out of these cuffs, control our own schedule like adults, and not be treated like slave labor? It's worth the risk."

"I thought you were trying to convince me it wasn't so bad here," I teased, but she just stuck her tongue out.

"That was before I knew we had a chance," she countered.

"Every three days," I thought aloud. "Thirty-six hours…"

Ardelle finished for me. "And then it's show time."

"I can get some of the guys to modify a set of the racks, make a space for you two to hide." He looked over at Mack's bulk. "It's not going to be comfortable, man."

"Nothing about this place has been. Why start now?" Mack deadpanned. "I wouldn't mind giving you a hand with that."

"I think Mack and I need to make things as routine as possible, head to our assigned jobs, pretend everything is perfectly normal."

"What? No." I could feel Mack's aggravation. "I don't think we should risk it. If we know they're coming, why should we make it easy for them, keep you in plain sight?"

"I'm siding with your man on this one, honey." Jado shook his head, then winced. "Ow!"

"Listen to her first," Ardelle insisted. "Zayda always has a plan."

"We know the ghosts only come at night, right?" Jado nodded, but Mack didn't move, kept his eyes fixed on me. "So we only need to hide at night. Act normal during the day, then disappear. It's just for two nights. That shouldn't set off any alerts, people get locked out of the dorms pretty often."

"They could already be on the way." Mack's voice was flat, but I could feel the frustration creeping in around the edges.

"We can't do anything about that," I waited. He was smart. He'd get it.

"Fine. We stick together at night. I walk you to the clinic tomorrow, I pick you up." His eyes pleaded with me. "I know you can handle yourself. But give me this, Zayda."

"You can stay here tonight," Ardelle bounced up, bustled around the room. "Right, my king?"

Jado laughed. "I'll get a couple guys to stay by the door."

"You wouldn't mind if I talked to them, too, would you?" Mack rose to his feet. "I'd like to see what sort of access there is to the area."

I watched the two of them wander out to the chaos of the Down Low. Unlikely allies, but, really, how much did I know about either of them?

Ardelle moved to the chair next to me, reached for my hand.

All of the bouncy bubbly was gone now, concern wrinkling her forehead.

"Now that they're gone, I need you to tell me honestly, Zayda. Does that man have some sort of hold on you? Is there something else going on?" Her eyes searched mine. "You're always so closed off, so vigilant. He's only been here for a day and already you're willing to put your life in his hands." Her fingers squeezed mine tightly. "Do you trust that man?"

Every shred of my training screamed 'no'. No one could be trusted. Let no one close to you. Every bit of my ego, bruised and betrayed, came out of the dark corners of my mind to rebuild the walls. No no no no.

I don't know why I whispered. "I do."

MACK

*B*efore we headed back out into the noise and commotion of the nightclub, I stopped. Jado cast a wondering look over his shoulder. "What's up?"

"Thank you for what you're doing for us. I know it's a risk for you."

He laughed. "Man, you're handing me a kingdom." He lightly socked me in the shoulder. "I may not have always made the smartest decisions, but I'm no idiot." He headed back through the curtains. "Besides, my babe would feed me my own balls if I didn't help Zayda."

Jado picked four of his guys, broad and burly, with the flat look of killers in their eyes.

"Nobody but me or Ardelle gets through to the back room, period. You keep this guy and Zayda safe, you're going to like the reward."

His grin was wolfish, almost familiar. Certainty struck me. I'd known someone else who gave orders in that easy, confident way. Maybe once we were out of this place I'd find him.

"Talk to you tomorrow," Jado said as Ardelle slipped out from the back room.

"Jado honey, would you go on for just a bit. I need just a couple words with our new friend here," she purred.

The minute they were out of sight, her easy smile fled and sparks flared in her eyes.

"Don't you hurt her," she hissed, her finger prodding my chest as if to punctuate each word. "I'm not fussy about what people did before they got here, that's pretty obvious. But you take care of her. Or so help me I will find a way to get to you, and you'll regret it."

At any other moment it would've been funny, the sight of her threatening me. But right now we were talking about matters of life and death.

More importantly, we were talking about Zayda.

"If I hurt her, or allow her to be hurt, I'll let you." It was the only possible answer. And the truth.

"Good." She turned and marched away. I watched her catch up to Jado, snuggle into him as his arm wrapped around her.

I SHIFTED the flimsy curtain behind me, wishing for something a hell of a lot sturdier. Three or four layers of permasteel would be nice. Out of the corner of my eye, I saw the guards Jado had set take their positions.

But I'd still rather have the permasteel.

Zayda still sat in her chair, playing with a long strip of fabric, weaving it back and forth between her fingers.

I dropped onto the floor beside her and she jumped as if she'd been lost in thought. Tension wrapped around her, tight as any binding.

"What's wrong?"

"Other than we're planning to break out of the prison that isn't designed to ever let anyone go unless they're hustled off in the middle of the night by ghosts? And that I might have just put the

CAGED

one true friend I've made up here in terrible danger?" She threw up her hands. "Nothing, why do you ask?"

I rubbed her arm with light strokes. Her muscles were taut under the skin, as if tied into knots.

"I think your friend is tougher than you realize. And she'd be hurt if you didn't let her help."

A small puff of laughter met my words, just a little, but it was enough to make me wonder what it would sound like, what it would take to make her laugh for real.

"You're probably right." Her face sobered again. "But we need to talk."

Her eyes went back to the little piece of fabric. She folded and unfolded it in tiny pleats between her fingers.

"Let's assume everything goes to plan. We survive the shuttle trip, they unload us somewhere on Orem, and we get out of the warehouse with nobody noticing." She pulled the fabric tight. "Then what?"

"What do you mean?"

"What do we do after we reach the station," she spoke slowly, as if trying to work through a problem, lay the issue clear.

"Once we're back on Orem, there's a," she paused, and once again I wondered how much she wasn't telling me. "There's a package I need to pick up. And then I need to take it somewhere. Alone."

I sat back on my heels and rubbed the back of my neck. Her tension was contagious. What would I do when I got back to Orem? If I could go anywhere, do anything...

"There's a place I need to go," the words spilled out of me before I realized they were on my tongue.

Zayda sat up straight, grabbed my hand. "Does that mean you remembered something, do you know what happened?

"No, it's just a feeling. There's someplace I need to go." I could almost see myself at the controls of a ship, plotting in a course for... I shook my head. I couldn't remember anything further, it

61

wouldn't come. But as soon as I had the chance, I was going to figure that out.

"So, sounds like we're in agreement." Resignation tinged Zayda's voice. "Once we get back to the station, we'll go our separate ways."

She headed to the privacy booth behind the screened-off bed.

"The bed certainly looks large enough for both of us. I'm not going to think about what Jado and Ardelle get up to in here."

"Good idea," I called after her, but my mind was far away.

Go our separate ways.

The leaden words sunk into my gut. I had assumed we would stay together after we made it to Orem. No reason for it. Maybe it was just because Zayda had been a part of my new life since waking up. It was hard to imagine going on to something else without her.

I stood up, shaking myself out of the melancholic mood. And that was stupid. Obviously, I'd had a life before her. And she'd had a life before me. We both would be fine.

Even if I hated it.

By the time I came out of the privacy booth, she had stripped out of her outer layers and curled onto the far side of the bed.

"I still really don't want to know the details, but, I promise you, this is much more comfortable than the deck floor we were on last night. Come on in."

I folded my shirt and draped it carefully over the back of one of the chairs before climbing into the bed.

She was right, this was better than the deck, hell, it was even better than the bunk in the dorm.

In the dorm. Oh, hell.

"Gozer," I muttered.

"What?" came the sleepy reply.

"Gozer, a chemhead, but in his own way he tried to be kind to me. He found a bunk in the dorms for me last night. I said I'd be back, and I haven't given him a second thought since."

"See if you can find him tomorrow at mess, easy peasy." She reached across the expanse of bed that separated us to rest her hand on my shoulder. "Tell him you got a better offer."

"Good plan."

She rolled over, her back to me. "Good night, Mack."

Zayda's touch still burned on my skin, her presence in the bed was almost unbearable. I remembered how she'd felt in my arms, the smell of her neck, the groans she'd made when I tasted her.

And through will alone I stayed perfectly still. "Good night, Zayda."

The dream began as it always did.

A blank room, walls of gray dimly lit from no source I could see. I lay on my back with my arms and legs outstretched, strapped down, immovable.

I had to get out. I had to get out. I had to get out. The refrain beat in my mind louder than my own heartbeat.

If I didn't, they'd be back. And, no matter how much I fought them, one day, maybe not today, maybe not tomorrow, but one day I would tell them what I knew.

The door slid open and I stopped straining against the bands. Too late.

As the tools powered up, I forced my mind blank, refused to hear their questions.

Where did they go? How do we find them? What message will call them all back?

I didn't fear the knives, or the shocks, or the torch.

The fear of telling them what they wanted to hear was far more terrible than anything they could do to me.

ZAYDA

ack's quiet groans woke me faster than any alarm. I reached for him in the dark, hoping that my hand on his shoulder would be enough to ease his sleep.

But this time the nightmare had dragged him deeper, its claws refusing to let him go.

I brushed the hair away from the sweat beading his forehead, his face clenched as his head whipped from side to side.

"Mack," I whispered. "Come on, honey, come on back to me."

But he couldn't hear me past whatever stalked him in his dreams. I straddled him, leaning over his chest to cup his face in both of my hands.

"Mack, it's Zayda. You're safe." Not that safe meant much on Minor, especially considering what we were planning.

But I'd bet nearly anywhere was better than where he was trapped in his own head.

I leaned my chest against his, desperate now to find a way to reach him, when suddenly he snapped awake, sitting half upright, his arms wrapping around me, keeping me upright.

"Zayda," he groaned and slumped back down, his face pressed into the crook of my neck, his breath coming in ragged gasps.

"Sorry about that, darlin,'" he muttered.

I moved to get off him, but his arms tightened around me. "Just give me a minute, all right? Sorry I screwed up your night."

He rolled on his side, carrying me with him. I stroked his back, relieved that he was back with me, more frightened than I cared to admit.

"What is it?" I whispered. "Does this happen every night?"

"I don't remember," his soft rumble against my skin was strained. "It's gone, fading like smoke when I wake. Someone wanted something, kept asking, demanding it..." He faded off. "I can't give it to them, Zayda. I can't."

I pressed a kiss against the top of his head, still stroking the knotted muscles at the base of his neck.

Darkness, this wasn't the time, but just the feel of his arms around me, his warm spicy scent, brought the memory of our little show 'distraction' last night to the front of my brain. The sensation of his hands upon me, his chest crushing into my breasts sent a twinge of warmth to my core...

I would've sworn that I hadn't moved, hadn't given any sign of my arousal, but I felt him stiffen against me.

"Zayda," Mack breathed against me, his voice sure and steady now. He licked at my neck and I moaned.

Like lightning, one of his hands cupped the back of my head, fingers knotting in my hair, bending my throat, opening and exposing me to his desires.

Every kiss, every nip, every touch dealt shattering blows against the wall of ice I'd wrapped around myself.

He rolled to his back, and once again I knelt above him. But this time, even in the darkness, I could sense his eyes fixed on mine, as tangible as his hands roaming my body.

He reached up, sliding his hand under the hem of my shirt, kneading strong fingers into the muscles on either side of my spine until I groaned in relief, stretching against him. Suddenly annoyed with all the extra fabric in the way of his hands, I pulled my tank off in one smooth motion, tossing it somewhere, anywhere, just away.

"Stop. Just let me look at you," he growled.

I leaned forward on his chest to drop a kiss on his chest. "Silly, you can't see me in the dark."

Before the words had left my lips, he sat up, his hands spanned my hips, lifting my breast unerringly to his mouth.

I gasped as he licked around one aching bud, nipping at it lightly before he switched to the other.

"I could see you in the middle of the Black, Zayda. You shine for me."

With his final words, he brought me back down, and through the thin fabric of my shorts I could feel the steel-hard length of him, straining against his pants.

Maddened, I couldn't help but grind just a bit against him. Sparks flew behind my eyes as his hands guided me, pulling me down harder, rubbing my clit up and down his length until I gasped.

Before I caught my breath, we had flipped again, Mack covering me, his elbows trapping me beneath him, but I didn't want to escape.

I ran my hands under his shirt, my nails down his back, and he hissed. "I never thought you were such an exhibitionist," he whispered in my ear.

"What?" I gasped. I knew those words. I knew what they meant. But in a sentence, right now, I couldn't get them to make any sense.

I reached for him again, but this time he pinned my hands above my head. Holding me still.

His breath caressed my ear with every word. "If we keep going, you're going to scream. And I plan to have my hands busy doing things to you, so I can't promise to muffle the noise."

His words, the promise and the threat of what he wanted to

do, what I wanted him to do, forced another moan that I pressed against the skin of his shoulder.

"Jado's men are right on the other side of that curtain." He kissed my neck, right below the ear. "Even if it kills me, we're going to stop now."

Awareness of our surroundings slowly seeped back into my consciousness. What had I been thinking?

"But Zayda," he whispered, as he nuzzled my neck and I arched up, desperate to touch more of him. "Before we go our separate ways on Orem? I promise we'll finish this."

His lips brushed mine with the lightest of kisses, the gentle contrast to our heated grabbling even more explosive to my shredded nerves.

I felt the muscles in his chest ripple as he moved to shift off me and I could have wept at the loss of contact.

"Yes," I murmured in agreement as I curled up on his shoulder. "I promise, too."

"Ready for a busy day, darlin'?"

Stretching, I snuggled into his chest, until his words and my location dawned on me. I twitched out of Mack's arms, frantically trying to recover my wits as I scooped up my tank top and scrambled into the privacy booth.

I leaned my head against the wall. Separate ways.

When I came out, I couldn't meet his eyes. "I'm heading to the clinic early." I pulled on my over-shirt, back turned to him. "Need to get those codes before Denon comes in."

Mack's large hands stroked my shoulders, and, despite myself, I leaned back into him. "I'll come with you and then meet the others at the mess." He pulled my hair out from inside my collar, smoothed it down. "Don't go anywhere alone." Mack turned me, caught me in his gaze. "Please, Zayda." His lip quirked up. "If nothing else, for the sake of the plan."

"For the plan."

At the door to the clinic, Mack gave my hand a final squeeze. "I'll be back at end of shift."

I knew there was no arguing with the determination writ large across his face.

"For the plan," I teased and headed inside.

To my surprise, Denon had spent the night with the burned patient, pulling his desk chair, not particularly comfortable but better than the other half-broken one, next to the cot.

The wounds were healing well. I made a surreptitious inventory of the oxygen tanks left. Despite the plan, I certainly didn't intend to interfere with the patient's treatment.

But my memory had been correct, there were plenty, even if we had another ten accidents before resupplying.

When I moved to check the levels of the current tank, Denon jerked awake.

I couldn't tell. Was the surprise in his eyes merely startlement at being awakened, or had he expected me to already be gone?

For a moment I doubted myself. What if those messages weren't anything about me? Certainly I wasn't the only person of interest to the governor on Minor that could be considered a bitch. Even I wasn't that cocky.

But the timestamps lined up so neatly.

The plan, Zayda. You have a plan, stick to the plan.

"Denon, if you've been here all night, take a break. I've got day shift covered."

He did his own check of the wounds and seemed satisfied. Maybe I had been wrong; he wasn't a great medic, but he did seem to care.

He rubbed his face with his hands. "Maybe at least to get down to the mess." He gave a long yawn. "Or maybe I'll crash for the morning." He stood, stretched. "I'll be back, at some point."

He headed out and my shoulders sank with relief. Not knowing the time of his return was a slight complication, but even having him out of the way for a little bit gave me a chance to get into that comm.

The file was right where it had been; obviously Denon hadn't noticed my earlier intrusion.

Good. After the incident on Orem, I'd begun doubting my own skills. As much as I hated to admit it, maybe I hadn't been betrayed. Maybe I'd set off some sort of alarm when I'd found the files. I forced the familiar spiral of my thoughts away. This wasn't the time.

Next step. There was no printer in the room. To manually transcribe all of the control codes for the cuffs would take considerable time, time I didn't know if I had.

But after we escaped, someone might start looking more closely at the access logs on this comm. Just writing the path down for Jado's electronics expert was risky - no way to be sure they wouldn't be moved.

I hated doing it, but there was nothing to be done except buckle down and start writing. I perched on the half-broken chair, swearing as it tilted beneath me. In frustration, I pushed it away and dragged Denon's chair over.

My eye caught on a black rectangle lying half under the cot.

A dummy tablet. Lots were scattered around the satellite, used as trade goods for favors, or drinks at the bar. They could receive, but not send.

And that was all I needed.

By midmorning, a steady stream of visitors to our patient arrived. Several I recognized as having been in yesterday, but I was surprised when a small, dark, pudgy man came up to where I was doing the daily inventory of medications.

"Thanks for looking after," the man paused and I realized he didn't know the patient's name. "Anyhow, anything I can do for you?"

He raised his eyebrows at my blank expression and then scratched his neck, drawing my eyes to the dark mark there.

The Skulls. Of course.

I glanced over to the inventory of slender oxygen tanks and flashed two fingers. Whatever this guy had been on the outside, he was quick on the uptake.

"You want me to move any of those empties out to the loading dock for the shuttle tomorrow? May as well get ,'em while I'm up here."

"I appreciate it," and we loaded up two more of the suddenly helpful visitors with empty oxy tanks - and two completely full ones.

As they loaded up, I slipped two of the thin hyperbaric balloons into the man's jacket.

And after that, all I could do was wait.

The hours slipped by, and Denon returned. "Zayda, go on. You may as well take a break."

I glanced at the chrono. Still hours before Mack's shift would end. "Nowhere to go," I shrugged. "Not exactly like I can take a walk." I slid the loaded tablet under my hand. Denon eyed it, and I scrambled, my words spilling from my lips before I thought it through.

"I thought I might read to him for a bit," I gestured to the patient. "I know he's pretty far under, but I figured it can't hurt."

His face relaxed. "Sure, good idea." After a few minutes of my toneless recital of the latest thriller, Denon logged out of his comm. "I'm going to get some more rack time." He paused by the door, an odd note in his voice. "I'll see you tomorrow, right?"

"Of course," I answered blandly. "Where else would I go?"

MACK

*A*t the compost pit, my two workmates from yesterday shooed me away. "Jado sent the word down, someone's gonna come and cover for you. You're needed on another project," the bald one said as he pulled on the work coveralls.

I fought my growl of irritation down. I didn't like not knowing what was going on, being sent from one section of the satellite to another.

But Jado had the resources that we needed right now, even if the control codes that we offered him would be more than a fair exchange.

Besides, I really hadn't been looking forward to getting into that mess again.

By the time I followed their directions, I ended up at a door at the end of a series of store rooms, guarded by yet another of the Skulls.

He eyed me and then stepped aside. "Jado said you were big, that I'd know you on sight. He was right."

Inside, an older man with the dark, toughened skin of someone who's spent most of his life planetside or somewhere with a high radiation count, came over and measured me.

"It's going to be a tight fit, son," he said as he turned back to his work.

"I'll manage. What can I do to help?"

"You know how to handle tools?" he asked, his doubt made friendlier by the slight smile on his face.

"Not at all. But if you need stuff lifted, moved, or held in place, I'm your man."

"That's always useful. Come on, we've got lots of work to do, and not much time to do it."

The day wore on endlessly. I couldn't believe how much time and care could be spent on constructing what was basically a long, hollow box.

The craftsman, Elsu, grinned at my obvious frustration. "Gotta make sure the weight balances. We don't know how the grow racks are unloaded on the other end. They might run over a scale, double-check that we're not shorting them. Never know, best to be sure and careful."

"My apologies, I'm just anxious." I hefted the next panel he pointed at and brought it over for him to shape.

"Don't blame you for getting nervy. You're taking a helluva risk."

"No more than the rest of you." A twinge of conscience struck. "Jado decided to put everyone at risk, didn't he, when he agreed to help us. Do you resent him for it?"

Elsu laughed. "Jado knows damn well we'd all kill for a fighting chance to be free. Die for it, if it came down to it." He made another cut, then carefully beveled the edge. "Rather not, of course."

Our work was interrupted by a group of men carrying an assortment of long, thin tanks.

A pudgy, dark-haired man nodded at the pile of tanks, then looked at me. "Your old lady's pretty smart. You keep her safe, and I'd lay money on her doing the same for you."

"I plan to." Thoughts of Zayda brought the memory of her skin under my hands to mind. Not the time or place, but the stray thought from last night re-crossed my mind.

"Hey, where would I find the laundry?"

Elsu looked up, bemused. "What, need an emergency load of dress uniforms pressed before you go?"

I shook out my jacket hem. "Nope, wouldn't know how to wear them. Just need to talk to a guy."

He stayed silent, waiting.

"Do you know Gozer?"

He whistled. "Son, he's got more wires loose than an old jump drive. Everyone knows Gozer."

"Maybe he's a little jumpy," I argued, "but he means well."

"Never said he didn't." The old man went back to his work, no doubt expecting me to do the same.

Worry struck. "Anyone give Gozer a hard time in here? I can't see him fighting back much."

"Nah." The welder handed me a sheet of permasteel to move to the other table. "Bad luck to mess with people like that. Need all the luck you can get up here." He stood and stretched shoulders that must have been stiff from a day of being hunched over. "Look, we'll get a message to him, if you think he's going to be worried about you. But I need you here, helping. Priorities, son."

I nodded, and got the next section of the rebuilt rack to be adjusted.

Priorities.

Elsu cut me loose shortly before the end of the day shift. "More help than I thought you'd be, to be honest."

I'd climbed in and out of the coffin-like enclosure throughout the day, checking the hidden latches, estimating the space Zayda would need curled beside me.

He tilted his head to the door, eyes still focused on one fine piece of work. "But you're edgy now, and it'll throw me off. Go get her, and save us both a headache."

"Thanks." I stopped by the door. It seemed such a measly word to offer, but I didn't have anything else. I went to get Zayda. Priorities.

She waited for me just inside the clinic door, obviously anxious to get out.

"I hate that place," she muttered as we headed down the hall towards the mess. "It's like a prison inside the prison." She straightened her shoulders and took a deep breath. "Denon's acting weird. He knows something is going on, but I can't tell if he's heard about what we're planning, or if he's just waiting for the ghosts to come get me."

The thought hit me in the gut and for a flash I wanted nothing more than to crush the spine of the man who would have happily handed Zayda over to those monsters.

I knew what they could do, I knew what they did do. And...

I stumbled in the hallway. No, I didn't, did I?

"You okay?" Zayda asked, her hand under my arm as if she could support me.

"A long day finding out I am not meant to be a welder, that's all," I joked, trying to put the eerie feeling behind me.

Before we turned the corner to the mess hall, Zayda stopped me.

"Here, hold this." She slipped me a dummy tablet like the man in the dorms had been reading. "It has all the information Jado's genius will need to take control of the station."

"Then why are you giving it to me?"

"Because if anybody tries to give us any trouble, they're a hell of a lot less likely to find it on you." She reached inside the sleeve of her jacket, pulling out a handful of small flat clips. "Turn around."

Zayda folded up the hem of my undershirt and secured it into a pocket with the clips, pulling and tugging to test its security.

"Suture clips," she explained. "There. With your jacket back down, I can't even see where the tablet is against your back." She squeezed my arm. "Not so great for hiding in small spaces, but you're handy to have around."

"Speaking of small spaces," I said as we entered the mess. "I'm glad to know you're not claustrophobic."

She raised her eyebrows but we didn't say anything else as we moved through the lines in the mess.

Word must have spread through the prison that something was going down. Several inmates went out of their way to walk by the table we occupied, pausing to glance at us, look us over, evaluate and weigh.

No one said anything, just nodded and moved on.

"Does everyone know?" Zayda whispered as she glared at the mound of greenish-gray goo on her tray.

"I suspect a lot more people than we realize are making our project possible." I put down my spoon. If we were going to be out of here soon, I'd eat real food on Orem. If not, well, I'd resign myself to a life of this sludge when it came up.

"You're right." Zayda pushed her tray away, obviously of the same mind. "And I suspect they're afraid of Jado enough to stay in line."

"I'm putting my credits on Ardelle," I answered, "I'm scared of her myself."

Zayda's laugh echoed throughout the mess hall.

THIS TIME we didn't bother with the pretense of drinks, just went straight back to the small apartment behind the Down Low to meet with Jado and Ardelle.

A stranger sat with them, an older woman, short gray hair framing an angular face.

Zayda stopped, looked her over. "You the techie?"

"Was," the woman's gravelly voice dragged out of her, surly, bored. "Before I got stuck up here and had all access removed."

"Have I got a present for you." Zayda smiled and slipped the tablet out from my shirt. She flipped to a certain page and handed it over.

The woman's eyes lit up and in moments the two of them were hunched over the tablet, flipping screens and muttering what sounded to me like babble, but obviously was a shared language between them.

"Think you can do it?" Jado asked.

The woman looked up, her eyes not entirely focused on him, still running through the codes in her head. "Yeah, this part is easy. But she got us a lot more. I need to think through some of it."

Zayda stood up, and I noticed she braced herself. I shifted to stand closer, and wondered what was coming.

"We have a couple complications."

Jado shook his head. "I really don't like that word."

"This wasn't avoidable. I used the hand scanner from the clinic to generate the frequencies before. But, if I try to leave the clinic with it, it'll trigger an alarm." Her hands clenched in frustration. "I tried to remove that section of the wiring, but even tampering with it would set it off."

Jado scowled and started to say something, but was interrupted.

"No problem." The gray-haired woman looked up from the tablet, eyes bright. "You just need a frequency generator?"

Zayda nodded. "Can you build it?"

"Yeah, sure, back in a few." The woman wandered off, still muttering schematics and codes.

"And there's something else we need to talk about," Zayda continued.

Jado started to speak again, but this time Ardelle cut him off. "And we'll figure it out, too. What's up?"

"Most of the cuffs are programmed to check for a pulse every ten minutes or so," Zayda explained. "In case someone dies in their sleep, or needs medical attention. Once we get them off, if we don't put them on someone else, they'll send a signal." She sat, and I stood behind her, hands resting on her shoulders. "I don't know how many layers of bureaucracy it would have to go through, but it wouldn't be long before it ended up in front of the governor."

Jado rocked back in his chair, thinking. "Is it possible to disable the punishment subroutine?" he asked.

"There's an override for that in the controls," Zayda answered.

"But if we keep ours on," I added, "the governor and his staff would be able to track us. Even if they can't use the shock to punish us, we can't risk it."

Zayda bit her lip, her finger tapping as she thought. "It's not ideal, but if we disabled the punishment subroutine, everyone could keep their cuffs on here until your tech is able to secure Minor from outside interference."

Jado nodded slowly. "Everybody's used to them, I don't expect it to take her too long to get it together."

"But what do we do about Zayda and Mack's cuffs?" Ardelle asked.

"It just needs a heartbeat, right? Any heartbeat?" Jado asked.

Zayda nodded.

"Fine, I'll put one on, Seig can wear the other. If the subroutine for punishment is disabled, not a big deal, right? And, if it's not, we're the best choices for being able to take a doubled dose."

Ardelle and Zayda's eyes met, but no one said anything. It was the best choice, but no one had to like it.

Before the silence stretched on too long, the gray-haired woman was back. "Let's give this a shot." She held up what looked like a random collection of wires wrapped around pieces of scrap circuit board.

"Never said it would be pretty, just that it would work. Gimme a wrist."

Ardelle bounced up. "Take mine off, even if it's just for a minute," she held out her arm, waiting. "I've had an itch for a week that I can't get at."

"In a minute, babe." Jado pulled her into his lap and stuck out his own arm. "On the off-chance there's an additional booby-trap stuck into these things, you're not getting hit with the shock."

The tech ran her homemade frequency generator over the cuff. Pressure mounted in the back of my skull with every second the high pitched whine continued. I clamped my jaw, determined to ignore it. Just when I thought I was going to have to leave the room, with a 'pop', Jado's cuff clattered to the floor.

We all stared at it.

"It really worked," and for once the lazy drawl was gone from his voice.

In minutes, we all had our cuffs removed, rubbing and scratching the abraded skin.

"They have to be replaced soon. I'm sorry," Zayda said.

"You don't have to be sorry for anything ever again as far as I'm concerned," the tech said. "Even just a minute of not being pulled sideways by that stupid thing is fantastic. I hate to put it back on, but knowing that soon it will be gone forever? We're good."

"What about the rest of it?" Ardelle asked "Do you think you can lock down Minor, keep the station from connecting with our system?"

"I can keep this?" the tech held the tablet up and Zayda nodded.

"Right now I'm at 86, maybe 87% certainty. I'll try to have a higher number by the morning." She wandered out again.

"She's never going to get to 100%," I said. "No matter how good she it, there's always a chance of failure."

"Sure," Jado's tone regained its swagger. "But I've never had those good of odds for anything. Doubt anyone else has, either. We'll take it."

"Well," Ardelle said, "I think we should all plan on an early start tomorrow. It'll take a while to get you into position and test the oxygen."

She stood up, tugged on Jado's hand until he followed her. "Have a good night you two!" She called over her shoulder. "Don't stay up too late!"

"That was... odd."

Zayda reached for my hands, still at her shoulders. "I think she's trying to give us some privacy before whatever happens tomorrow."

"Mack?" The tentative note in her voice struck alarms. "I'm worried about tomorrow. What if the trip is longer than we figured? What if the tanks don't last?"

She spun in the chair, her eyes wild with worry. "We don't know how they unload on Minor, what they check for, or..."

"Hey, hey." I reached down to stroke her hair. "We've done everything we can. The hidden compartment is built down to the last micron to get us through. No one is expecting a breakout. As far as anyone knows, it's impossible."

Zayda didn't say a word, but I could see her lost in lists. Nothing I said reached her. "Come on," I leaned over the back of her chair, lifted her over it. "Let's go to bed."

"What?" The change of topic caught her off guard. "Mack, I'm not sure if..."

I sat her on the bed and turned to the privacy booth. "Just to sleep, darlin'." The door to the privacy booth closed behind me, and I called out over my shoulder. "Besides, who else is going to keep me safe from the nightmares?"

ZAYDA

*I*t didn't work, of course. But this time I was already nestled against him, my back curled into his chest, when I felt his arms tighten against me. "Mack, wake up," I whispered, rubbing his forearm. A deep sigh, as if something was letting go, and he relaxed.

"Thanks." He dropped a kiss on the top of my head.

"Fair trade," I mumbled. He'd stayed awake until my mind quieted and I had drifted off, as safe with him as anywhere I could possibly be. But now the endless lists of things that could go wrong spooled through my mind again. Was I going to get us killed? Was our escape going to bring retribution down on the entire satellite?

"Stop thinking," Mack commanded. "Plenty of time for that once we're in the compartment."

And surprisingly, I did.

~

WHEN THE LIGHTS brightened for day shift, I woke in the bed alone.

"Mack?" I called out, confused. And was then angry with myself. We'd known each other for two days, by the end of today I'd never see him again. So why was it so bewildering to wake without him beside me?

I slipped out of bed and found him on the other side of the screen. The chairs had been pushed to the side, and he flowed through a series of stretches, positions that hovered on the line between looking uncomfortable and lethal, his eyes closed, and his movements sure.

When I stepped past the chairs, he froze, eyes snapping open.

"Where did you learn that," I breathed.

He shook his head. "No idea. But it seemed like a good idea to get some stretching in this morning. You may want to, as well. We're going to be pretty cramped in there."

We skipped the mess, even though the bitter kaf in the hall called my name. We both knew we'd be better off with nothing in our systems during the trip.

I paused, uncertain of where to go first. "I think if I don't show up at the clinic, Denon will just assume I was taken last night. I'm sure he's been expecting it. Let's just go, get ready to load up."

Mack said nothing, just looked grim as he checked outside the small apartment, and then held the curtain aside for me. The guard had changed during the night.

"Big day, eh?"

"Everything goes to plan, it'll be a quiet day, actually." Mack shook the man's hand. "Thanks."

Ardelle met us in the corridor outside the Down Low. "You've got to see this," she whispered. "Elsu has done an amazing job."

I might have been expecting a buzz of activity at the loading bay, but, at first glance, everyone looked bored, waiting for the shuttle to arrive so they could get on with this task and get back to their day.

Eight strong men and women lounged on overturned crates. One side of the bay held a line of what looked like shelving units, except each shelf burst with greens, tubes running down the sides in a confusing tangle.

"Wouldn't it make more sense for the station to have us harvest the greens and package them here?" I asked, confused.

Ardelle smiled, humor sparkling in her eyes. "Probably, but, apparently, so many people want the absolute freshest food possible, and are willing to pay for it, that they do the final stage there." She shrugged. "Saves us time and labor, and they send back the empty racks on the next shuttle."

"Of course, if things go as we hope, that won't be happening for a while." I added. "This will be the last they get, won't it?"

"Until they're willing to deal. We can always make more racks if we need them, but there's more than enough to keep Minor fed."

Each of the racks had an enclosed cabinet at the bottom.

Mack tapped one as we got closer. "That's where the water filtration and nutrient system goes. And that's where we'll be. The plants won't be as happy, but it's a sacrifice we're willing to take."

I looked at the cabinet and then back at Mack. "How exactly are you going to fit in there?"

"Like a pretzel," he grimaced. "But it works, believe me. We tried it out a dozen times yesterday. It'll work."

Jado and the tech whose name I never caught last night came into the room, her arms waving wildly. While I wondered if Jado was taking in every bit of jargon, he was certainly smart enough to know where she was going with things. He looked happy, so I'd bet she'd raised her prediction estimates for a successful takeover. Good.

Lights flashed and a low siren wailed.

"Incoming shuttle," Jado called out to the group. "Everybody behind the line."

We hurried to make sure we were behind the scuffed yellow line painted on the floor, walls, and ceiling before the field snapped into place.

Through its shimmer, I could see the landing bay doors begin to open into the cold blackness.

I shivered, and my hand crept into Mack's. "I don't think I've ever seen this before. It's so easy to forget we're floating in a thin shell of metal in the middle of space."

He squeezed my hand, and I noticed he didn't seem fazed at all. Whoever he was, wherever he'd come from, it wasn't the first time he'd seen this terrifying sight.

The shuttle glided in, and we could feel its engines cut even as the loading bay doors sealed behind it.

The fields dropped, and Jado's crew rushed to the slowly extending loading ramp, ready to check for incoming prisoners before loading the racks.

Our attention was so fixed that none of us heard the rush of oncoming footsteps.

"You bitch," was the only thing I heard as my hand was ripped away from Mack by a rough grip on my shoulder.

I had no time to notice anything else before a stinging blow landed on my cheek and I stumbled backwards.

Larko crouched over me, features contorted with rage. "You're still just station trash, you-"

Mack leapt on him with a low growl, cutting off anything else he planned to spew.

The force of impact carried the two of them back, away from the shuttle, where everyone had frozen to their spots.

I shook my head and climbed to my feet, ears ringing. "Larko, what the hell is your problem?"

What I saw tore the rest of the rant from my lips. I stopped talking and rushed forward.

Mack held Larko's throat in one hand. The creep's hands scrabbled at Mack's fingers, his feet kicking air, his eyes beginning to bulge.

Jado stood next to Mack, voice even, ignoring Larko's quickly reddening face. "Hey, man, you got him. We'll take him from here. No one's going to hurt her."

But Mack gave no sign of hearing him.

I slipped under Mack's arm, wrapped my arms around his waist, and rested my head on his chest.

Void, I could hear his heart beating loud and fierce, even as one arm wrapped around me, held me closer.

"Mack, I'm right here. I'm fine." He didn't move. "Please put him down. Let's go, please?"

Gradually, Mack lowered Larko's now limp body to the deck. His other arm came around me and I could hear his breathing ease, become regular.

Jado wandered over to Larko's limp form, prodded it with his foot. "Think we figured out what to do with those cuffs. Nice of him to volunteer." He flashed a slightly nervous smile at Mack, who still stood unmoving. "Good job you left him with a pulse."

The tech popped our cuffs off and replaced mine on Larko's right arm, and Mack's around one of his legs.

"Maybe we'll just see how many he can carry," Ardelle spat.

A commotion at the door to the loading bay had Mack spinning, shoving me behind him. The sound of an odd, high-pitched voice was the last thing I expected to snap him out of it, but he suddenly relaxed.

"Let him in," he called.

A skinny, older man shuffled forward, hunched over a bundle of fabric he held to his chest. His eyes lit up when he saw Mack.

"I heard, I heard the whispers," his eyes slid back and forth, weighing the trustworthiness of our band of rogues and scoundrels. "You'll need something, I made it, I did."

With a little bow, he handed me one of the bundles. I turned it over in my hands, then gasped, shaking it out to flow before me like a slice of midnight, shaped into a halter necked dress with a flared skirt. "It's lovely!"

Beaming, the little man handed the second bundle to Mack. As

Mack unfolded the black pants and short sleeved green shirt, he patted Mack's arm, chattering all the while. "Can't go down looking like us, can't do it. Need to look like them, blend in."

If you knew the clothes had been refashioned from standard regulation uniforms, you might be able to tell how he'd done it, but no one passing by on a glide on Orem would give us a second look.

"These are amazing!" I couldn't help but hug the little man. "Thank you so much!"

He started patting my arm, now. "I was a tailor, I was. Had a wife and little girl." His bloodshot eyes grew misty. "All gone now."

Ardelle wrapped her arm around his thin shoulders. "Would you like to be a tailor again?" she asked softly.

He blinked, looking surprised. "Can I?"

"Things are changing around here. I'm going to have all sorts of projects for you. Why don't you wait for me, and we'll head back together and talk some."

He beamed at her. Maybe things could get better up here after all.

"Okay, boys and girls, let's get moving." All of the grow racks had been loaded except for one. Jado stood by it, while an older gray-haired man slid open the short panel at the end, revealing the empty chamber within.

Mack nodded goodbye to his tailor friend. "We'll need these. Even before we get there, we could use the padding."

I looked at the compartment dubiously. "How do we even get into this?"

"Yesterday we realized that backwards is the way to go." Mack handed me his change of clothing and proceeded to back into the crate. It couldn't have been comfortable, he would have to keep his knees bent at an awkward angle and his shoulders hunched together the entire time we were inside.

But he was right, there was no other way.

I padded the clothes around his head the best I could and then gave my new dress to Ardelle.

"I want that back in a minute," I teased. "No running off with it."

She hugged me fiercely. "We'll get you down there, you'll do your whatever it is, and then you find a way to message me, got it?"

Ardelle waved away my unspoken words. "Don't tell me what it is you're doing, I don't need to know, it doesn't matter." Her face softened. "Just let me know you're all right."

I nodded, throat too tight for words. Then I backed into the dark box and pressed against Mack's chest.

Our position was a mockery of the way we had slept last night. Instead of taking comfort from each other out of choice, we were wedged in as tightly as possible by necessity.

Ardelle tucked the dress under my head. "The racks are secured to the shuttle deck, but I don't know how much bouncing around there's going to be."

I twisted, saw where the thin lines came in from the two oxygen tanks that had been added underneath the bottom rack of plants. The tubes fed through the top of our compartment, ends dangling over our heads, each hooked into the end of one of the hyperbaric envelopes.

Gently, I unfolded one, exposing the wide opening on the underside. In the clinic, we'd position that over the wound. This was not the normal procedure.

"This might hurt when you pull it off." Adhesive backing uncovered, I positioned the opening over Mack's nose and mouth, carefully checking for gaps around the seal.

Ardelle watched intently, repeating the same process for me.

The bags didn't inflate, they didn't in the clinic either, but with a few tentative breaths, I knew oxygen was flowing. If the box had been airtight, we could have just pumped the oxy in, not bothered with the masks. As it was, this would do.

"Time's up." Jado crouched down next to Ardelle. For once, he seemed at a loss for words. "Good luck," he finally said, and slid the panel back into place.

Immediately the loading crew rolled us up the ramp, stomping and chattering.

I could hear clamps lock around us, and the clang of the loading ramp retracting.

And then the only sound was the reverberation of the shuttle's engine echoing through our tiny chamber.

We were out.

MACK

*W*eightlessness.

For all of our planning, we somehow hadn't prepared for this.

As the shuttle left the satellite's gravity field, Zayda drifted from the bottom of the compartment. Wedged in so tightly, I didn't move at all, but could feel the lift in my gut. And, since Zayda was in here with me, she didn't go particularly far, either.

"I don't like this," she whispered, her voice muted by the tough plastic.

Odd. Weightlessness was comfortable, almost soothing, to me.

But from the way she lay, muscles tight with tension beside me, I could tell it wasn't the same for her.

Our environment limited the range of my arms, but that didn't stop me from pulling her just a tiny bit closer.

"We're not going anywhere, at least," I joked. "We couldn't be more secure if we were strapped in a jump harness."

There had to be something to take her mind off this.

So far, she'd been unwilling to tell me what her mission was once we reached the station, and I hadn't pressed her. Her business.

There was another topic that should be fair game.

"At first, I thought that guy, Larko, was just harassing you because he was a jerk. That you had turned him down, and he didn't handle rejection well." I searched for something clever to say, but maybe it was best to stick with the basics. "It was more than that, wasn't it?"

Zayda sighed. "We knew each other as kids. We might've been friends back then, really. Maybe more like allies. It wasn't really safe to have friends growing up, to get too attached."

She faded off and I stroked her upper arm with the one hand that had a tiny range of movement.

"Well, you know all my secrets. At least all of them that I do."

The tightness in her shoulders loosened against my chest. "That's true. Not that that's saying much, of course."

Spooned against me in the dark, she couldn't see my answering smile, but she continued anyway.

"Since you don't remember Orem, you probably don't remember the Cilurnum stations. Orem was built by a private company, if I'm remembering right."

Zayda recited a lesson learned long ago, no emotion to the story, just bare facts.

"The Cilurnum stations were built by the Empire as a boundary, the edge of expansion. Under the old Emperor, the Imperial troops withdrew to maintain order nearer the center. The Cilurnum stations were left in the hands of anyone who could keep them. Some stayed more lawful than others."

The situation sounded familiar. I didn't remember learning this, but, somehow, I knew she was right. This was the universe we lived in, somewhere on the Fringe.

"Station three might not have been so bad, if you were in one of the upper levels. But the Lowers were a nightmare. We thought it was normal to have packs of kids roaming the back corridors of the decks, sorting through piles of refuse for anything to eat, anything to wear, anything to keep you safe at night."

Her tone shifted, voice threaded with sadness. There wasn't a way to comfort her, and I couldn't change the past, anyway.

"Larko was one of the kids in my pack. We weren't close, but he grew up just as hungry and scared as I did."

"I don't remember anything about my childhood," I told her in the long silence that followed. "But I think there was at least someone who cared for us. I'm sorry there wasn't someone for you."

She squeezed my arms where they wrapped around her stomach. "But that's the thing Larko was so angry about. There was someone. He just came late, and, in the end, he only took me.

"A man came down to the Lowers. For the longest time, he just sat in the open squares, watching." She gave a muffled laugh. "He looked so posh to us that every kid tried their hand at robbing him, but somehow he knew all our tricks, stayed a step ahead.

"Then he started to bring down food. He'd set it down on a bench, go sit on another, and just watch. Some of us thought it would be poisoned, or drugged. But we argued, wanted it. We were so hungry all the time.

"Finally, I couldn't stand it. I asked what he wanted."

She stopped, lost in memory again, and I thought of all the ways this story could end. A man of comparative wealth and power, trolling for desperate children. Rage burned in my muscles, but it wouldn't help Zayda now.

"He said he was looking for me. Oh, not me in particular, but someone who was brave enough to ask questions. He asked if I wanted a new life, was I willing to work for it. And that day we left the Lowers, and I never went back."

Trapped in the compartment, there wasn't enough space for me to hit something, and even if no one was in the shuttle's hold with us, yelling was a bad idea. So I worked very hard to keep my arms from tension and my voice level as unwelcome images flashed through my head.

But I had to ask. "How exactly did he expect you to work for it?"

"Not like that," Zayda slapped at the back of my hand. "At the time, I might've agreed. But no, he taught me, trained me. Gave me an education and a future. And now I need to get back to him, to my job."

A completely unreasonable wave of jealousy washed through me. He didn't sound like a lover, more like a father figure. It was just the unequal balance of power that bothered me, I told myself. Sure.

"So, what happened to Larko?" I asked.

She collapsed a little in my arms. "I never saw him again, never even thought about him. I was so focused on everything I needed to do, to learn. Everything Stanton Grene taught me."

Her voice faded to the barest whisper behind the muffling plastic. "Maybe I should have tried to go back, do something for the other kids, but I was holding on by my fingernails to what I had, to a future I had no right to expect. Turning around to look backwards, I was afraid I would have fallen."

I strained to hear her next words.

"I didn't see Larko again until my first day on Minor. Didn't even recognize him until he started hassling me."

Her words slowed, and she faded off into silence.

"Zayda?"

"Mmm?" She answered sleepily.

"Are you doing okay?"

"Just tired, maybe we should nap the rest of the way."

A spike of fear hit me. "Zayda, are you sure your air is flowing?"

"I think so."

But I wasn't so sure. I pulled my shoulders back as much as possible to give my hand a little more room to move, then slid my fingers over Zayda's face, pushed her sweep of hair away, and felt for where the tube entered the plastic envelope.

It was still attached, but something felt wrong.

Micron by micron, I contorted until I could reach the tube connecting to my own makeshift mask.

Damn it.

On the connection to my own mask I could feel the faintest vibrations through the tube where the oxygen flowed.

But there had been nothing from Zayda's.

I didn't know if her tank had failed or the tube had loosened in the rack above us, but it didn't matter.

Her body lay slack in my arms, unresponsive.

Finding out exactly what had gone wrong would have to wait. Right now, she needed air.

With a quick jerk, I pulled the tube from my mask and worked back over to hers. Switching the lines with one hand in the dark with limited range of motion wasn't the easiest thing, but her limp form added drive to my focus.

As soon as the lines were switched, she started to revive.

"Hey, sorry for dropping off like that. How much longer do you think it will be?" Her groggy voice grew stronger with every word.

It would be so easy not to tell her. But if the trip didn't kill me, she would if she found out.

"Hopefully not much longer because we've had a little complication." In as few words as possible, I explained the problem.

"Mack, you need the air, too." All drowsiness was gone for her voice now. "Even if you-" She bit her words off.

I knew she was right, but, so far, I felt fine. "Maybe the stories of keeping the shuttle without an atmosphere were just that, stories."

She shook her head. "We can't trust that. We're going to have to just alternate."

For the rest of the journey, we switched the one tube back and forth between our masks.

Until finally I couldn't feel the movement of air from the second tank, either.

"Mack, I think...."

"I know, darlin'."

This time, there wasn't anything I could do other than stroke her hair while she went to sleep.

Finally, I heard the hiss of gas being released in the shuttle's cargo bay all around us, and gravity pulled us harder onto the floor of the compartment.

We had landed, and the cargo ramp was extending, breathable atmosphere rushing into the shuttle.

But was it too late?

"Zayda, wake up."

No response.

I pinched her skin lightly until she stirred in my arms, then my own stupidity struck me. I ripped the envelope from her face, then covered her mouth with my hand as she let out an angry "Ow!"

I couldn't risk a word, but in seconds we both heard steps, muted conversation all around us.

Slowly, I moved my hand and together we waited in the dark, grateful that our gifts from Gozer hadn't shifted too much during weightlessness as we were bounced and rolled down long corridors.

Finally, all of the noise around us stopped.

I listened as steps faded, people moved down the corridors and away. I refocused, trying through hearing alone to get a sense of the room we were in, but nothing alerted me.

"I think they're gone," I whispered, and pulled the adhesive off my own face, then blinked in shock. "That really hurts!"

Zayda elbowed me. "At least you knew it was coming!" But I could hear the smile in her voice.

"You ready to get out of here?"

"If we can still walk." She reached up to unfasten the hidden latch and slide the panel open.

It didn't move.

Threads of panic wove around the edge of her voice. "I think we have a problem. Something must have shifted while we were weightless," she hissed.

As wedged in as we were, I couldn't reach the panel without putting an elbow in Zayda's face. "I can't reach. You have to try again."

Still nothing.

"We can't get stuck now," she said. "I can squeeze down farther, see if you can move your arms more."

At any other time, Zayda squirming down my torso would have been distracting.

Now, I just wanted to get us both out.

"That's far enough," I muttered. "Let's hope I'm right and there really is nobody in earshot. "

I could only get one arm partially above my head, but it was enough to hammer the panel with three sharp blows.

Zayda and I both heard the click after the third one.

"Stop," she whispered. "Let me try again."

This time, the panel slid free.

We wiggled out, and every muscle in my aching legs rejoiced when we finally lay stretched out on the hard floor of a dark warehouse, gasping

As soon as I could, I stood and grabbed my new clothing. "I'll head that way while you change."

In the dark, thoughts of Zayda, only separated from sight by a thin screen, danced around my mind, diverting me from a more pressing question:

What the hell was I going to do now?

The urge to get off Orem had only grown. Not to leave, exactly. I needed to go somewhere, some place.

Coordinates I couldn't speak burned in the back of my mind,

waiting for my hands to flip the controls of the ship that would take me there.

AND THAT WAS THE CATCH. I'd have to find a job, earn enough to get a ship, or find someone who let me do courier runs long enough to have the ability to detour for a bit.

But I'd find something. That would be the next step.

I finished dressing and waited.

Nothing from Zayda.

"Everything all right?" I called softly.

"No." Her voice was flat. More aggravated than scared, but definitely not happy.

When I reached her side, she was fully dressed, prison uniform neatly tied into a nondescript bundle.

Her hair had fallen out of her braid during our trip, spilling like black water over her shoulders.

The dress fastened behind her neck, skimming over her torso, leaving her shoulders bare, other than the covering of her dark hair. The skirt flared out at the hips, and I imagined how it would flow around her as she moved.

Zayda glared at her feet.

"What's wrong? It looks great." Great was a vast under-statement.

"The dress is fantastic. However," she pointed down.

I had to admit, the clunky black prison-issued boots we'd all worn on Minor seemed out of place under the graceful dress.

"You look beautiful, and like you can kick ass. Both things are true, so what's the problem?"

She huffed a little, then sighed. "It's a small thing to be worried about after we're actually free. Just a tiny complication."

I stuck my hands in my pockets. "Jado slipped me some credits before we left. Not a lot, but surely there's a place we can find a pair of shoes."

Zayda muffled her laugh. "Ardelle did the same for me." Her tone sobered. "I wonder how it's going up there."

I took her discarded bundle of clothing, added it to mine, and took her hand. "The two of them make a pretty good team, don't you think?"

Slipping through the aisle of goods waiting for their next destination, she followed me through the warehouse. "Better than I realized."

"Let's trust them to get their job done. We've got our own to figure out."

My memory might be spotty, but I was sure I'd never before said the next words:

"First mission, shoe shopping."

ZAYDA

 e eased the door to the warehouse open and
 glanced around.

In the half light of the warehouse district, I turned to Mack, then stopped, my breath nearly taken away. Back on Minor, he'd just been another big, tough guy, in a crowd of them. Sure, some bigger, some tougher, but he didn't stand out from the crowd.

Here, in the carefully crafted outfit that Gozer had created for him, he looked like a wild beast, amusing itself with a masquerade before it reverted back to nature.

The fabric fit smoothly over his broad shoulders, although I suspected he'd have to be careful not to bust a seam when he moved.

The civilian clothes should have helped him blend in, instead he just looked dangerous, like a barely sheathed blade.

He'd been so surefooted in the warehouse, moving around crates and racks and, in one case, even a pile of scattered tools an idiot had left in the middle of the walkway without a single misstep.

Here, he just looked lost.

"No memories of this place at all? I whispered, squeezing his hand.

"Nothing. I don't think I've ever been here."

At the next intersection of core doors, I glanced around.

"What are you looking for?" Mack said, his voice pitched so low I could barely hear it.

"Either glides to the next level or a public recycler."

He led us surely to the left, and soon the crowd thickened and the corridor widened enough that small vehicles zipped down the middle of the stream of people.

"The noise made it likely," Mack answered my raised eyebrows.

Before we got to the glide, I'd disposed of all our old clothes, putting just one at a time into each recycler as we passed. I wanted to get rid of all of them at once, but scattering them seemed like a better plan.

If anyone interrupted the disintegration schedule, the trail might lead them straight to the glide we'd used, but it seemed less likely that someone would see a pair of pants, or a jacket, and realize what the entire outfit would have been.

At the top of the glide, I looked around and relaxed. "I know where we are."

"That's good," Mack muttered. "I have no idea."

No one seemed to notice us; probably no one even caught the discrepancy between the ugly boots and the gorgeous dress. But it felt like I was waving a red flag over our heads with every step.

Luckily, the solution to the problem was close to my goal.

I smiled up at Mack. "Ready for an adventure?"

"I'll take you anywhere you want to go."

His words didn't mean anything. I knew that. They couldn't. But, just for a moment, I let the easy warmth spread through my chest. It couldn't hurt anything to pretend for a bit. Nothing more than a woman and her handsome man out for an afternoon stroll.

Two glides and a lift later we fought the crowds of the bazaar.

"Aren't there other places for you to find shoes?" Mack grumbled as we slid between groups of other shoppers.

Or, rather, I slid, he loomed until people got out of his way.

"PROBABLY, but nowhere as cheap. We don't know how long those credits need to last us. Besides, people here are good about not asking too many questions."

I found a booth I'd been to before, run by a tiny, hunched-over old man of indeterminate age. His gap-toothed smile welcomed us as we wandered towards his table.

Not many had stopped to examine his wares. Their loss. I had found several good bargains here when I had been trying to blend in on a tight budget before.

"Hey, Missy," he reached over the table and patted my hand. "You've been gone?"

"Maybe. Just not around."

He didn't ask. One of the great things about the bazaar. Nobody asked too much.

Most fabricator goods didn't last long enough to be saved, passed on, sold again and again.

It was easier just to fab new things, break down the old whatever it was and start fresh. But some people would always find a way to turn an extra credit.

I tapped a pair of light gold sandals that looked close to my size. "How much?"

The old man's eyes flicked down to my boots. "They'll will look better than those things."

"Any chance of a trade?" I asked hopefully.

"No, Missy." A nice man, but nobody's fool. "But I'll get rid of them for you."

Our business concluded swiftly. As we stepped back into the flow of traffic, I felt considerably less conspicuous.

"Where to next?" Mack asked. His stomach rumbled. "Dinner would be nice."

"I promise, one more stop, and then we'll find dinner. And then..."

He rubbed his thumb over the back of my hand, and every fiber of my body remembered my promise. One night.

But first, business.

"This way."

I led him deeper into the bazaar. The booths were smaller here, more cramped, the shoppers a little more furtive.

"Do I even want to know what we're doing down here?"

"Sometimes a girl needs shoes, sometimes a girl needs spare parts. The nice thing is, you can find just about everything down here, if you're willing to look at all the dark places."

His eyes roamed over each booth, every merchant, trader, and shopper.

"Anyone, anything you recognize yet?"

"Nothing. None of it looks familiar."

"That doesn't mean you're not from Orem," I tried to keep my voice light. "Maybe you didn't have a good reason to come down here."

"I'm not from here. I don't know why, but I know that."

As we headed for Klayson's booth, I wondered.

Suspects that had been mind-wiped never regained their memories.

Ever.

Mack's certainties, the flashes of memory that had come back to him, were unheard of.

It was possible maybe this was all just a long con. Maybe he hadn't really been wiped and was just a crappy actor, planted to get the disk.

I glanced up at him, as he scanned the hallway, missing nothing.

He probably was a pretty bad actor, to be honest. Too direct, too impatient.

But I didn't think he was lying. Anyone who knew about the mark a wipe left would have been able to tell him to just play dumb, don't mix it up.

That meant something unheard of was happening.

And maybe Mack was in more danger than I was.

It was late afternoon by the time we made it to Klayson's. Unlike his neighbors, he didn't leave a sampling of his wares on display. Tall drapes blocked most of the space from view, with only an empty table out front.

If you were here, you knew what you were looking for.

I rapped my knuckles on the empty shelf and waited for him to emerge.

"Just a minute," an old woman's voice sang out.

I frowned.

That wasn't expected, and, right now, I didn't need unexpected.

A woman hustled out, thin, back bent with age. Dozens of tiny braids spilled from her headscarf, framing her deeply lined face.

But her eyes were bright and quick and she assessed us as she emerged from the canopy.

"Hello, children, what are you looking for today?"

"I'm looking for Klayson, actually."

Mack must've heard the tension in my voice. His stance, always wary, shifted just a bit, even more prepared for a fight.

She looked between us but, instead of being nervous at Mack's presence, as I'd expected, smiled broadly.

"I'm very sorry, then. Klayson had a big order, so headed off to do a little scrounging. I expect him back in a few days." She let out a deep laugh. "Hope so, I promised him I'd keep an eye on the booth for him, and it's seriously interfering with my own bad habits."

The smile stayed frozen on my face as my mind spun.

A coincidence?

Possibly.

Klayson scavenged for interesting bits of hardware, abandoned tech, the more esoteric variety of parts.

But the timing worried me.

"I don't suppose there's any chance he left a package for me."

The old woman shook her head. "As I don't know your name, dearie, I couldn't tell." Her bright eyes must have caught that something was wrong, as her voice softened. "But he didn't leave any package. He'll be back in a couple of days. Is there a comm where he can reach you?"

I stepped back from the table.

"No, we've…"

The words wouldn't come. I'd been so focused on getting back to, or getting to, Klayson's booth and finally completing my mission, I hadn't thought of contingencies.

I'd failed.

Again.

Mack stepped up, his hand rubbing soothing circles between my shoulders while he spoke to the old lady.

"We've been on a bit of a bounce-about, haven't set up local comms. Would you have recommendations for guest quarters? I think we'll be on station for a few weeks."

Her sharp eyes appraised us both. I was certain she'd turn us away, for the paupers we were. But something about us must have struck a chord.

"I think I've got just the place for you."

His arm wrapped around my waist. "We're not looking for much, but clean and private are high on my list."

"Let me see to a few things," she laughed. "Wait there."

She disappeared back under the canopy and I turned to face him.

"What are you doing?" I whispered, my anger at myself threatening to bleed over to him.

"We've got to stay somewhere until your contact comes back," he replied, maddeningly reasonably. "Any place you normally would go to is going to be under watch as soon as they realize you've escaped."

The bone-aching weariness I'd been holding off by focusing on getting off Minor returned, doubled. I let him pull me to his chest, stroke my arm while he explained.

"I don't know anything here. Let's see what she's got in mind. Can't hurt, right?"

The old woman appeared with a carry bag slung across her body.

"Come on," she said and bustled away. "Business has been terrible, anyway, and sitting in one place makes me bored."

She headed through the bazaar and Mack and I scrambled to keep up with her.

As we emerged into a quieter quarter, Mack frowned.

"Ma'am, I'm pretty sure you're going to say no, but I have to ask anyway. Can I carry that for you?"

She stopped, looked back at us. "I was right, you'll do well." She turned and continued on.

"And you're right, too. No, you can't. Klayson trusted me to watch his stuff. Even if it's boring bits and bobs." She turned a corner, and a young man darted out of her way. "Call me Granny Z, everyone does."

"Alright, Granny Z. Where are we going?"

The buildings on this level were rundown, but clean. The air smelled off a bit, and I wondered if they could use a few of Ardelle's plants.

She snorted. "Chances are good if you're looking for Klayson, you've got your own business. And your business is private."

Granny Z glanced down and pointed at Mack's boots striding beside her. "And I know where those come from."

I froze, began to move back into the depths of the bazaar, away from this old woman who saw far too much.

107

Mack squeezed my hand, and I relaxed just a bit.

"Really, ma'am, we need to know where you're taking us."

She stopped and turned back, clearly exasperated. "I'm not turning you in, if that's what you think. If Klayson was holding a package for you, he trusted you. And that holds weight with me."

"But you'll need a place to wait for him, and I've got something that will work. But there are rules."

I couldn't breathe, couldn't move. Just waited.

"First, don't lie. Second," she paused, pulled on a braid and nodded, "that's pretty much it, actually. If there's something you think you can't tell me, just say so. Don't lie to me."

She turned back and we followed, both of us in a bit of shock.

"Can't abide liars, never could. My grandson can't seem to do anything but. I'd love to blame it on those friends of his, but, somehow, he just turned out bad from the beginning."

The residential hive was so old it seemed to be sliding back into whatever materials it had been originally formed from.

A handful of kids came spilling out the front door at our approach, circling Granny Z, tugging on her skirts until she shooed them back inside.

The ground floor was surprisingly bright. Granny noticed my confusion as I searched for lighting panels and found nothing.

"Too expensive," she said sharply. "Look over that way."

I followed her finger, to see a cluster of tiny trillian lights. Eyes wide, I re-examined the room with new focus.

They were tucked everywhere, lending a gentle glow to the large space. But trillian lights, that was a luxury I had seen only in the highest of Agency offices.

What were they doing here?

A thin woman stepped out from the back of the room, but her smile fell when she saw Mack.

She stepped away, as if ready to run, when Granny Z patted her arm.

"Marga, dear," her sharp voice soft, gentle. "I brought home a couple of friends."

A ghost of a smile returned. "More strays, Granny? No matter," she said, turning back into what smelled like a kitchen, "I got a good deal at the bazaar today. We can easily feed two more 'friends'."

We followed Granny Z up two flights of stairs. "Lift works, most days, but it's better to keep your legs strong."

I dodged another child as it ran down the steps, chased by a playfellow. "What happens if one of them breaks their skull on this?" I asked, only half joking.

"Learning experience," she said shortly. "Here you go."

The room inside was small but tidy, lit brightly with the unexpected trillian lights.

"The control panels for the lights and the necessaries are here," she tapped the wall. "Nothing fancy, but clean. And private."

I looked at Mack, weighing how much we should tell her. Wondering how much she already knew.

"Thank you," was all I finally said. "We appreciate it."

I held out my hand but she pulled me into a hug. "Everything looks better after dinner and a good night's sleep, dear." She pushed away, eyes twinkling. "You know, I don't even know what to call you."

"Some days we're not sure either." Mack leaned against a wall, and, for the first time, I saw how tired he was.

"That joker is Mack."

He bowed in acknowledgment.

"And I'm Zayda."

Her gales of laughter brought the children down the hallway, but she waved them away.

"Of course, you are, honey. Of course, you are."

MACK

I stared at the door as it slid shut behind Granny Z, then turned to Zayda

"I know I don't remember much, anything, really, from before I turned up on Minor. But..."

She shook her head and sprawled back on the wide bed that took up half the small room. "No. That's not normal. Maybe not dangerous, but not normal at all."

The bed looked secure enough, but I sat on the edge gingerly, testing to see if it would support me before I lay back beside her.

"Do you think we can trust her?" Zayda turned over to face me, dark eyes wide. "She knows too much."

I brushed the hair from her face, thinking. Nothing about the old woman smelled of fear or deceit. "I think she just has an odd sense of humor," I finally decided. "Besides, you said the bazaar was a good place to find people who didn't ask too many questions. She seems like she'd fit right in with that crowd."

"True." Zayda's gaze fixed on the cluster of lights at each corner of the room. "I just don't like mysteries."

"I'll try not to take that personally."

She rolled on top of me, eyes bright and alert, back with me instead of lost in thought. "I make an exception for you, as a favor."

I ran my hands up her bare legs under her skirt, fingers kneading her supple skin until she sighed with satisfaction.

"What other favors would you be willing to grant me?"

Hands on my shoulders, she lowered herself until her lips brushed mine. "I did promise you a night." Another featherlight kiss, then she nuzzled into my neck. "And I do keep my promises."

I moved one hand, pulling her towards me, deepening our kisses, drinking the taste of her in. Her scent, her touch, soothed the last of my nerves, still stretched thin from our trip. With every groan I drew from her, the nightmare of holding her limp body faded.

We jumped at the knock on the door.

"Granny saz dinner's ready and come down after you wash," a child's voice called out, followed by a furtive whisper. "Don't be late or she makes you stand in the corner." The pattering of feet down the stairs proclaimed the departure of our messenger.

Dinner was a noisy affair, but I'd take the laughter and chaos of the children over the bravado of the mess hall any time.

After the meal, we offered to help with the cleaning, but Marga waved us away. "The children have chores now, don't they?" Amid much muttering, the table was cleared and the sounds of washing up started from the back.

"Let us at least pay for our portions," I reached for the credits in my pocket.

Granny Z shook her head. "Credits come and go. Favors are a much better barter item."

"We don't know how long we'll be here," I started, but she cut me off.

"I'm old. Plan to be older. I can wait, if needed." Granny Z pushed up from her chair and headed upstairs.

"If you go out, don't stay out too late," she called over her shoulder.

Zayda and I glanced at each other, amused.

"Nothing you can do with each other could shock me, children," she turned at the landing. "But it's not safe after full dark. Don't be on the streets if you can help it."

Marga came back, arms full of a sleepy child. "The viewport on this level is lovely, and pretty close, if you want to take a walk." She glanced at me. "I'm not sure if there are any other places I'd recommend, unless you were looking to burn off steam."

That made no sense, but Zayda patted my arm and shook her head. "He's not prowling for a fight, promise. The viewport sounds perfect."

We strolled in silence along the narrow streets, following Marga's directions. This sector of the level was quiet, but the rumble of a crowd sounded far behind us.

Zayda's fingers curled around mine, warm and soft, the fabric dress swishing around her knees with each step.

"Are you alright here?"

She stopped, confusion wrinkling her forehead as she looked up at me. "What?"

A pale woman with tangled dark hair staggered past us, then disappeared between two buildings. I tucked Zayda closer to me, wanting her near.

Words had never been my strong point, but I tried again. "Is this too much like where you grew up?" That was a stupid question. I never should have started down that path, but dinner had reminded me of Zayda's story of lost children, lost or forgotten.

"Void, no." She wrapped her arms around me, rested her head on my chest. "The kids look happy there, loved." We resumed our walk, my arm around her shoulders, fingers idly rubbing where the dress exposed her skin.

"There was none of that on my old level. At least, none that I found."

I pulled her tighter to me, but, no matter how I racked my brain, there wasn't a good response.

THE OLD OBSERVATION chamber was empty, the air still and heavy.

Perhaps people who lived on this level in this sector had other things to concern them this late at night. People who didn't live here never knew about it.

Which was a shame, the broad, transparent plexi was barely scuffed, and endless pinholes of light danced all around us.

Zayda went to the plexi, tapped near one of the brighter stars. "That's Lisa.B-1. Its light helps keep this place going."

I wrapped my arms over her shoulders, studying every cluster, each pattern, waiting for recognition.

Nothing came.

Zayda leaned back into me, her own arms twining up mine. I tucked her head under my chin. "I'd forgotten how much I used to like looking at the stars as a girl. All the ports on our level were blocked up years before. Sometimes I'd sneak to one of the upper levels late at night and just watch, imagine what it was like when the Empire was young, when people could make their own choices."

Choices. The word echoed between us.

"What do you think is out there?"

"Home." I'd said it without thinking, I didn't know where it was. But it was out there, somewhere.

She whirled in my arms, eyes alight with questions.

"I think. I don't know. I don't think I've ever seen a chart heading oriented from these coordinates. But I need to get out there, find it."

Zayda put her hands on my chest, staring up, her face serious.

"Tomorrow you're going out to the docks to find a ship, aren't you?"

Just the thought of leaving her brought a physical ache. But... "Unless you want me to wait until your package comes back."

She bit her lip, and, again, I could see the endless lists of impossibilities rolling behind her eyes. "No. That wouldn't be fair to you. And besides..."

Zayda fell silent, but she didn't have to say anything further. Her secrets stood between us, as always.

"Well, then." I bent over, breathing in her scent.

She stretched up on her toes to flick her tongue against my lips. "I guess this is our night."

With her words, the dam inside me broke.

Our night.

If I had only one night to touch her, to taste her, I would devour every inch.

Bending over her, I grabbed her ass with one hand, cupping the other behind her head to support her as I licked and nipped my way down her throat. Her hands clutched my shoulders as I pressed her back, supported by my arms.

"Mack." The sound of my name, her voice breathy with need, spurred me on. The swell of one breast fell free from her dress, and greedily I pulled it into my mouth, holding her tight against me as she shivered, moaning with each careful nibble of her tight rosy bud.

Her hands clawed under my shirt, the heat of her fingers branding my arms, marking me as hers.

I lifted my head to stare at her in wonder. Nothing was as beautiful, nothing as alive as my Zayda, with her clever mind, and now her lips parted, open for me to plunder.

She gasped as I took her mouth, and met every thrust of my tongue with her own, soft, wanting cries making my cock painfully hard.

"We should go somewhere else, darlin'," I whispered into the

ELIN WYN

shell of her ear as I lightly bit the delicate lobe. Her squirms, her whimpers set every particle of my being aflame.

"What?" Her lashes fluttered, brow wrinkled as she fought to focus. "Why?"

"Because elsewhere there's a door, and a lock." I set her down carefully before me, then tucked her breast back into the neckline of the dress. I couldn't help but caress her through the fabric, one last tweak to the nipple before we headed back.

She stiffened, eyes unfocused. With a snap, a wicked smile crossed her face.

"Two can play at that game, darlin'." She reached forward, sliding her hand down my length, which was straining against the confines of the fabric.

"Zayda," I growled, fighting for control.

"Yes." Her eyes flashed, and she repeated the stroke, but, this time, slower, harder.

With a muffled howl, I tore her hand away, spinning her around until she was pinned between my body and the plexi, facing the void. I pinned her wrists above her head with one hand, the other fisted in the fabric of her skirt.

Face buried in her neck, maddened by her aroma of adrenaline and desire, I slowly ground into her ass.

"Is this what you want?"

"Yes," she hissed, and pushed back against me.

Taking advantage of the gap between her body and the plexi, I slid my hand around her hip until the V of her thighs was microns from my fingers.

"Mine." I curled my fingers around her mound, the thin-stretched cloth only the slightest barrier.

She shuddered against my chest, and I rubbed the wet fabric in tight circles until her breath came in gasps.

"Hey! What are you doing in here?"

I pivoted, blocking Zayda from view. An older man, clothes disheveled, peered in the door.

From his hesitant motions, uncorrected vision blurred us from his sight. He shuffled further into the chamber, head swinging from side to side.

"We're leaving," I rasped.

I swung Zayda into my arms, and we headed back.

ZAYDA

"*H*ang on."

That was the only warning I got before Mack started running. Night shift had started while we were in the viewing chamber, but my eyes were still filled with stars, my mind reeling at Mack's touch.

What had just happened?

I wasn't a virgin, but I'd never lost control like that. Never wanted to.

But my skin still smoldered where he'd held me, stroked me.

An aftershock rippled through my core, forcing a low moan of need from my lips.

Mack's arms cradled me tighter as he picked up speed. I buried my face into his chest, drinking in the smell of him.

Unable to stop myself, I tasted the sliver of skin I'd exposed.

"You're going to kill me," he rumbled, moving even faster through the corridors. "Be still, or I'm going to find the closest alleyway, passersby be damned."

I was half tempted to test him.

I half wanted him to do it.

But I lay quiet in his arms, fighting the urge to squirm just the tiniest bit.

～

As we approached the silent residential hive, I wiggled.

"Zayda," he warned.

"Let me down, we don't know who's still up."

"I don't care." But, grumbling, he lowered me to the street outside the door. I gave myself a quick check-over to make sure everything was covered, then moved to re-fasten his shirt.

"Careful." Mack held my wrists, golden eyes narrowed.

"Behave for five minutes." I slipped my hands free, continued to fasten his shirt, ignoring my own heated pulse. "Once our door is closed, I'll make it worth your while."

It was a good thing we took those moments outside, for, as I reached for the hive door, it slid open.

Mack stepped in front of me, but it was only Granny Z.

The twinkle in her eyes betrayed the bland expression. "Glad you're home safe, children. Go on up to bed now, I'll lock up behind you."

We stumbled over our thanks in embarrassment, both anxious to get upstairs.

"Have fun, children," she laughed behind us and I felt my cheeks flame.

As the door slid closed behind me, I leaned against it, hands covering my face. "Well, that wasn't awkward at all."

Mack stood over me, his broad hands running up and down my arms. "I get the feeling she's seen and heard it all before."

His hands slid down my arms, continued to my back and then, in one swift motion, scooped me up so that our eyes were level.

The heat in his words rekindled the spark within me, and I wrapped my legs around his waist, running my fingers through his short-cropped hair. "Where were we?"

"Right here is good." I kissed him, biting at his lower lip, desperate to taste more of him.

I felt his hand at the back of my neck, fighting with the clasp of my dress. "I like the way this looks on you but I want it off you, now."

"Wait," I squealed and reached behind my back to undo the fastening. "Right now, it's the only clothes I have."

But he was silent, staring at me as the fabric crumpled down around my waist, baring me to his gaze.

I squirmed away from his intensity. "Let me get the lights."

"No." His voice was raw, rough. "I want to see all of you."

He lowered me to the bed and, as I pulled the dress over my head, he began to work down my body, kisses and light nips mixed with strong, languid strokes until I writhed at his touch, barely able to tell one from the other.

His thumbs hooked at the sides of my panties and in moments I lay bare, exposed before him.

"Come here," I whispered. One by one, I undid the fastenings of his shirt until his wide-muscled chest lay exposed to my touch.

I ran my fingertips down his sides, following the lines of the muscles of his abdomen as they disappeared into the waist of his pants.

With a sharp intake of breath, he shed the shirt, tossing it to the floor instead of his usual neat folds, then stretched out beside me.

"Arms over your head."

"Mack, what..." I trailed off in the face of his burning gaze.

"I've behaved. You promised to make it worth my while."

One hand clasped my wrists, holding them to the bed, while the other traveled lazily up the inside of my thigh.

I squirmed away from the featherlight touch, but he pinned my leg with his own, keeping me open and exposed to him.

At the first brush of his hand against my clit, I came off the bed. He covered my mouth with his own, swallowing my shout, even as he matched the thrusting of his tongue to the rhythm of his fingers below.

The sensations washed over me until I felt stretched like a balloon, every nerve exposed, ready to shatter.

With a final thrust, he ground the heel of his hand into my mound, and I exploded, the stars from the viewport all I could see.

When my breathing finally evened, I was curled, nestled in Mack's arms, the soft glow slowly fading.

"I thought I was supposed to make it worth *your* while," I murmured.

His soft laugh rumbled in his chest. "That was very much worth my while."

I wiggled against him. "That doesn't seem fair to me at all."

"I got what I wanted, I promise."

I reached down and stroked the hard length of him, felt him jump in my hand. "I don't think that's quite the case."

He groaned as I slipped out of his arms to lay beside him, running my fingers down to the base, back to try to circle the head with firm strokes.

"Tell me you already have everything you want from tonight," I whispered.

I licked my lips, watched the iron control in his arms twitch, and knew he was mine as surely as he'd taken me.

Dropping my head to his stomach, I kissed my way down, ever closer as I stroked him.

There was no warning.

Just a quick flip of motion, and he lay on top of me, his breath panting and eyes wild.

"Zayda, you don't know what you're doing."

I locked my legs around his, guiding him towards me. "I know you," I breathed and lifted my head to kiss him.

Still he refused to move.

Slowly, I ran my tongue across his lower lip, inviting, daring him. "One night."

With a shuddering lunge, he sank deep inside me. Every nerve I thought had been wrung out by his previous attentions flared as I panted, adjusting to him.

The slow rhythm built to a crescendo, drowning, overwhelming me, until I clutched at him as my only solid point in the world.

Every thrust battered the shards of my control, until I broke apart once more. Frantic to keep myself from screaming, I bit into his shoulder.

At the touch of my teeth to his skin, he froze, and then shattered, gripping me to him until, exhausted, we tumbled to the side in a tangle of limbs.

He kissed my forehead as I curled under his shoulder. "I don't think I'll have any trouble sleeping tonight, darlin'."

"I can't imagine either of us will."

I waited until I was certain he was asleep, fairly certain the nightmares wouldn't come, then gathered my clothing and slipped out of the room.

I paused at the door, dimming the lights. I hated this, but there wasn't a choice. I slipped out the front door of the hive, hoping I'd be able to get back before he woke.

Swiftly, I retraced our steps from before, back to an old public comm unit we had passed on the way to the viewport chamber.

I didn't have any credits on me. I wouldn't need them.

The comm number was one I'd never be able to forget, and I tapped my fingers, waiting impatiently for the connection to finally be made.

I was about to give up, try again at the next chance, when finally the screen cleared and the lined face of Stanton appeared from the static.

"Zayda?" he asked. "Where the hell did you go, kiddo? When you went dark, I damn near went out there myself."

Limp with relief, I checked in with my superior.

I passed lightly over Mack's details. Just a guy who'd been useful to help bust me out.

That's all the Agency needed to know.

"Do you need to come in? I can have a pickup there in no time at all."

I smiled. That was Stanton, tough as nails, but soft for his trainees when it came down to it.

I never wanted to disappoint him.

"No. I'm safe enough. I'll ride it out, wait for the package to return and then get out."

"Where did you hide that thing anyway?" He yawned. "Sorry, kid, this old man keeps earlier hours than you do."

"It's somewhere safe enough." I hated talking over open comms. "Just not in reach for a few more days."

"Well, take care of yourself. Don't go dark again, kid."

After he winked out, I touched the screen where his face had been.

As I hurried back to the hive, my thoughts were still on our brief conversation. Stanton had been as much a father to me as a trainer, a handler. The one person in the Empire I could trust implicitly.

What about Mack? a quiet voice from the back of my head asked.

I shoved the thought away. I was sure I could trust him. Mostly sure. But my first loyalty had to be to Stanton, the Agency, the mission. That was all I knew, all I had been trained for.

I repeated the line to myself over and over in the hope the refrain would quiet the small, insistent voice.

But when I turned the final corner to get back to the hive I stopped, frozen in my tracks.

Mack stepped out of the shadows, waiting for me.

"It's not safe out here. Where did you go?"

I could feel the anger rolling off him in waves. I took a step back and shock crossed his face.

"Do you think I would hurt you?"

"No."

But the damage had already been done.

"That's it. I don't know what to do. When I touch you-" he broke off. "It doesn't matter."

"Mack," I reached for him, but he pulled away. A sharp pain stabbed my chest, and my arm fell, lost.

"Just stay here until day shift." He turned his face away from me. "The door to the hive will unlock, you can go in and be safe."

He was right. I had chosen the instant I'd left our bed. Even if I didn't feel like I had any other options.

"What will you do now? I whispered into the darkness.

"Same plan as before. Find a ship, get the hell away from here."

Away from here, and away from me.

There was nothing left to say. We waited as the dark hours stretched before us.

The lights had begun to brighten for day shift when a muffled scream broke the stillness and we both jolted to our feet.

"Stay here," he snapped and tore towards the sound.

"Like hell, I will," I muttered and chased after him.

I lost sight of him in the twists and turns of the district, but another scream guided me.

A pale woman struggled with two black-uniformed men as they dragged her into an alleyway.

Mack launched himself at one of the attackers, knocking him away from the woman. The two grappling figures rolled away down the half-dark street, the sounds of their blows echoing.

The other dark figure stood in the shadows, unmoving.

I looked around for anything to use as a weapon and found a long, thin pole.

Without much confidence in its strength, I swung it wildly at the head of the man still holding the woman and heard a sickening crack.

Metal snapped in my hands, and he turned towards me, releasing her to slump against the cold deck.

"Get away from her, you bastard," I said and swung again.

He caught the pole easily, wrenched it out of my hand, and threw it away with a clatter. As the lights of the level turned up another notch, he stepped out of the shadow.

He. It.

The ghost.

The story had been laughable up on the satellite, but backing away from its looming shape, I couldn't think of a better term.

Flat black uniform that covered the entire figure, but it was no uniform I'd ever seen, nothing I'd heard of in training. The rumors were right, there was no face. Instead, it wore an opaque helmet, the domed shape oddly disproportionate to cover a human head.

Icicles crept up my spine, and I scrambled back to get away from it.

"Get down!"

At Mack's shout I fell to my back and rolled away without hesitation.

The second figure flew through the air, smacking into the wall next to where the first helmeted shape stood, hard enough that lights flickered on in the residential hive above.

"Are you hurt?" Mack pulled me from the ground and, for a moment, I felt the warmth of his arms before he released me.

I shook my head, and together we turned to watch the ghost rise as if nothing had happened to it.

"Stay behind me."

Stepping beside him, I brushed his arm. "Not happening."

But as the level clicked to the full brightness of day shift, like smoke, the ghosts disappeared into the night.

Mack started to follow them, but I called him back.

"Please," I forced myself to meet his eyes. "Help me get her back to Granny's, and then do whatever you want."

MACK

I picked up the blonde woman, her thin form weighing almost nothing. Her head lolled back, and Zayda gasped.

"Isn't that the woman we saw last night?"

A quick glance confirmed it. We'd seen her before we arrived at the viewport. Before Zayda's touch had made me feel whole, only to have her leave and shatter everything again.

She walked beside me in silence. The woman stirred in my arms, then shrieked, fighting with me.

Zayda rushed to her, as I lowered the woman to the ground, still standing ready to support her.

"It's alright, it's alright." Zayda held the woman's arms, searched for reason in her face. "He's one of the good guys, I promise. Nowhere safer you could be than with him."

The touch of her gaze on mine was like a kick in the gut. I believed her when she said it. Then why had she left our bed?

"Those men," the woman shuddered. "Those things…"

"Yeah, tell me about it. Let's get you somewhere safe." Zayda kept her arm around the woman's shoulders and I fell back to follow them.

I'd keep my word. Wait till they were safe inside of Granny's. And then... The future stretched black and blank in front of me, just like my past.

I thought of the woman's abduction, the fight against the helmeted figure, the wrongness as I touched it.

There was something there; I knew those things in black. But the memory slipped away even as I reached for it.

We reached the residential hive to see Granny already standing in the door, waiting for us.

"Is there anything you don't know?" Zayda's voice held a forced lightness.

Granny's quick eyes flicked between us, even as Marga wrapped her arms around the frail woman, bringing her inside.

I stepped back onto the walkway, ready to lock the door on the last few days. Lock the door on Zayda.

Granny paused on the doorstep.

"You two, wait for me." Her voice sounded twenty years younger, commanding.

"I need to head over to the docks, the earlier I get there, the earlier I'll find a berth."

Granny's gaze narrowed. "Last night I told you I'd rather have a favor than credit. I'm calling it in now."

The door closed behind her and Zayda slumped against the wall.

I fought to keep my voice even. "Are you hurt?" I shouldn't care, right?

"What were those things? What are they doing here?" She sounded lost.

I didn't put my arms around her.

It wasn't long before Granny came bustling out the door. "Come along, children. I have a favor I want from both of you, and then, if you like, we'll call it even."

We passed through the edges of the bazaar, and Granny Z glanced at Zayda's crinkled dress.

"That's a lovely outfit," she said, her voice gentle. "Might want to talk to your tailor myself one of these days. But you might want something more suited to travel, where we're going."

"Travel?" we asked in unison, but she ignored us and stopped by a booth filled with clothing and general gear.

Granny negotiated a quick transaction with a much younger man whose gaze at Zayda's form while he estimated her size made my fists clench.

In minutes, Zayda stepped out from behind the curtain, dressed again in plain black pants and a light gray shirt.

Too close to her uniform from Minor, if anyone had asked me. But the cut of the fabric was softer, not the unflattering boxy form.

"Just as lovely, child, and now a little more practical."

The young man smiled as Granny patted his cheek and we were off again.

We followed her up and down glides, shifting levels and sectors, and from Zayda's quick looks around, I wondered if she was as lost as I was.

Before long, she confirmed my guess. "I don't think I've ever been to this section before."

Granny laughed. "Not surprised. Private docks. Not a lot of public traffic." She kept walking, but the question seemed to have broken her silence. "When I was young, my family was going to marry me off. A wealthy man, and a powerful one, but old. And I'd never met him. Didn't love him. Ended up running away with a scoundrel and a rogue."

Twisting and turning through corridors, she stopped with her hand over a lock plate. "We had a good life. He left me a lot of memories, and this."

She opened the door and stepped through.

Lights clicked on overhead one by one, the sequence filling the chamber with brightness, all trained on a long silver shape.

I followed Zayda into the room, and, for the first time since our meeting, all of my attention was ripped away from her.

"It's beautiful," Zayda breathed.

"She," the old woman answered. "She is."

An antique runner, sleek and deadly, with curves out of a pilot's dream.

Granny didn't move any closer, but her eyes caressed the ship. "She's *The Queen*. My husband's ship. I haven't taken her out in years, not entirely certain my old bones are up to the G-forces anymore. But I have her checked out pretty regularly, whenever I find a pilot I think I can trust."

She snorted.

"Paying the berthing fees is the only thing my worthless grandson does that I approve of."

Zayda ripped her eyes from the ship to look at Granny. "*The Queen*." Zayda's tone made me turn. "What was your husband's name?"

Granny Z just shook her head and smiled. "Nobody important, just to me. Anyhow," her voice cleared of memories, "that's the favor I'm calling in. Take her out, give her a good run, and bring her back in one piece. A good ship's not meant to sit still."

I ran my hand over the hull. "How do you know I could even fly her?"

"I'm old, not stupid. Try again."

Void, this was everything I had hoped for, dropped into my lap. But with one complication.

I looked over at Zayda then refocused on the gleaming lines of *The Queen*. Much safer.

"Do we both need to go?" I tilted my head towards Zayda. "She might have other plans."

"Well, child? Do you?"

"I'll go, if you'll have me." Zayda's voice was flat, even, expressionless.

Fine, if she could handle it, so could I.

"Do you want us to leave now?"

"Darkness, no. I'd rather you didn't crash her the first time out. Neither of you slept nor had breakfast." Granny turned away. "Missing sleep, that's not that much of a problem. Breakfast should never be skipped. Come on."

Zayda brushed my arm as I passed her on the way out. "I'll keep out of your way."

I took a deep breath, kept going. "As far as I'm concerned, you won't be there at all."

GRANNY INTRODUCED us to the proprietor of a little hole-in-the-wall curry shop and ordered for us. "You can find the way back to *The Queen* now, can't you, children?

"Yes, ma'am."

Zayda nodded, eating her food with a distant look, tapping her ring finger. I knew that expression, she was thinking about something, puzzling something out. And I hated that it wasn't my business anymore.

"Can we take her anywhere?"

"Don't crash her, try not to get into a firefight, don't be gone too long."

I blinked. "No battles. We can do that. I'm not sure how long we'll be gone, should be no more than a station cycle or two."

Granny pushed up from the table. "That's fine. I keep her restocked and fueled." She winked. "Never know when you'll need to make a quick getaway."

Zayda looked up sharply, but didn't say anything.

After Granny left, I finished my bowl. "Definitely better than we got on Minor. Don't think this is where our fresh greens ended up, though."

Zayda smiled faintly. "I know you don't want me to go with you. I can stay down here, disappear. She doesn't need to know."

I snorted. "That old lady knows everything. I need that ship, and we owe her. And you owe me."

Eyes lowered, she nodded. "When do you want to go?"

"Now's fine, unless you need to do any other little errands."

I was being a dick. But I had to build some space between us, or the next time she disappeared...

No good thinking about that. I just wouldn't let myself get attached again. Shouldn't have in the first place. I waited for her to finish and then paid the smiling woman for our meals.

"Friends of Granny Z, you can come back anytime." She disappeared into the back of her booth, effectively dismissing us.

"Ready?" I turned away from the table but waited until Zayda had stood before leaving the shop.

All the way back to *The Queen*, I walked half a step in front of her to keep my hand from reaching over and wrapping her fingers around mine.

Still, I watched her, as her curious gaze took in every level, every sector we crossed. But still she seemed distant, resigned.

I guess she, too, had decided things were better this way.

We entered the codes for *The Queen's* dock and I walked around the sleek silver hull again.

"I've never seen anything like her." Zayda stroked the graceful folds over the outer hatch.

"I don't think I have, either. Whatever happened to me, surely I'd remember something like this."

Now that I had a ship, the compulsion to head to the unknown coordinates pressed harder in my skull. I rubbed the side of my head, avoiding Zayda's worried glance.

"Come on, let's check out the inside."

Runner class ships like *The Queen* don't have a lot of extra space, just enough for the cockpit, basic stores, and a drive.

I walked towards the cockpit and Zayda dropped to the decking, tapping it until she pulled up a panel.

"What are you doing?"

She glanced up from the compartment.

"Figured before we ended up in space, it wouldn't hurt to see what sort of machinery we had under the hood. I'm not much of a mechanic, but I know the difference between a flux and an impulse drive."

She ducked back down and I nodded.

That was good.

Wasn't sure I did.

Entering the cockpit, I smiled. *This* I knew.

I sat down, ran my hand over the controls. I could fly *The Queen*. I could fly her all the way home.

I couldn't be certain that the instruments arranged in the elegant panel before me were in the exact order I'd worked in before, but the function of everything was clear.

Almost everything.

One set of controls sat to the side, and no matter how I imagined using them, I came up blank.

"Mack," worry threaded through Zayda's voice. "Could you come back here for a minute?"

I raced to her side, ready for disaster.

"No." She put her hand on my chest to calm me, then pulled back as if she'd been burned. "It's not an emergency, just an issue."

I wanted to grab her hand, instead focused on keeping my voice even. "What sort of issue? Do we have a problem?"

"Not exactly a problem. But I've never seen this before." She pointed to a spinning ball of golden lights trapped in a web of silver that sat in what I assumed were *The Queen's* engines.

"Never seen it at all before, never seen this configuration. It's a bomb? Help me out here."

She stuck out her tongue at me.

"It's not a bomb. I promise I would have started with that." Her attention returned to the puzzle before her. "What we have here is a fully functional folded drive, embedded in a flux engine." Her fingers tapped her leg to a rhythm only she could hear. "I think we might want to do a few test jumps to a very empty space before heading to wherever you're going."

"Why?"

"Because, if this is what I think it is, we could end up appearing in the middle of a sun."

Yup. That counted as something between an issue and a problem. Not something we were equipped to handle, though.

"If we needed to know what it was, Granny would have told us, right? Let's assume she doesn't want us to wreck this beauty. How are we on fuel? I know she said it was stocked and stored, but she wouldn't be the first person to get scammed."

Zayda raised her eyebrows. "I don't think many people scam her. Not more than once. But you're right, let's make sure this isn't the once."

Quickly we determined the stores contained enough food and fresh water for a two-week trip, maybe more if we were careful. As well as a disturbingly comprehensive medical kit.

"When we get back," Zayda said, "I think I want to ask her a few questions."

I laughed. "Good luck getting her to answer them."

By the time I called flight control and got our departure path off the station arranged, we had settled back into an easy truce.

I reminded myself it was just that.

A truce, temporary.

Zayda settled into the copilot's seat. "You promised me you knew how to fly this thing."

"I guess we'll find out."

Carefully, I followed flight control's recommended path, deliberately going no faster than an antiquated glide.

I snuck a glance at Zayda. Her eyes were fixed straight ahead and she gnawed on her lower lip. Clearly an excess of caution wasn't making her any more comfortable.

"Let's go."

And, with that, I kicked *The Queen* into gear. She moved like a dream, hyper responsive to every flick of the controls.

"Now, this is more like it." Zayda's eyes were bright and excited.

I could smell her adrenaline in the air and, for a moment, my concentration was lost.

"All right, let's see what else this baby can do." My hand hovered over the unfamiliar controls. "You say this thing can fold space, pop us from one sector of space to another without any time spent in warp?"

She was back to gnawing at her lip, but she nodded. "I think. That's what it looks like. I've heard rumors of such things being put together. Never seen one.

"Mack, where we're going... How long would it take us to get there with just regular jumps?"

My hands paused. "I don't know."

She reached over the space between us and squeezed my hand. This time, I didn't break off contact.

"Then let it take as long as it takes. Punch in the coordinates, and let's find out where we're going."

I closed my eyes, saw my hands moving over the controls, not this panel, but one close enough. Didn't think, didn't try to pull the memory into focus, just did it.

I felt the hyperdrive kick in.

I looked at the readout. "Looks like it will be a couple of hours before we arrive. Granny's certainly getting what she wanted. A nice solid workout for *The Queen*."

Zayda's finger had started tapping imperceptibly.

"No."

"What?

"Stop thinking, stop wondering about Granny."

"But aren't you just dying to know?"

"No. I have plenty of mysteries without adding her in. And, besides, you need to sleep. Take a shift on the rack, try not to think about anything, and I'll wake you when we get there."

Wherever there was.

ZAYDA

*I*n my dreams, I tried to run towards something. I couldn't see what it was, but I knew I wanted it more than anything, but my feet were tangled in a sticky mess. Long cords wrapped around my arms as I tried to free myself, but, whatever I did, I was trapped.

"Hey, darlin'. Zayda, we're almost there."

The dream released me as soon as I felt the touch of his hand on my cheek.

I sat up and he stepped back from the narrow bunk.

The cold weight I'd carried in my chest all day got heavier, but there was nothing to do but carry on.

"Be right there." I nodded towards the privacy booth and Mack headed back to the cockpit.

I splashed water on my face, rebraided my hair, and took a selfish minute to stare into the mirror.

Good.

At least I looked as crappy as I felt.

Normally, I could tell myself that whatever the job was, I'd get through it. This is what I had been trained for. That the Agency, that Stanton, had saved me and that's where all of my loyalty should be.

This time, the words were like ashes in my mouth. Bitter and useless, and all I had left.

I slid into the copilot's seat and fastened my harness. Mack's tension filled the cockpit.

"Ready to see what's there?"

He nodded, jaw tight, and then punched us back into normal space.

What the hell?

We emerged in a meteor field, and only Mack's reflexes kept us out of the way of an oncoming chunk of ice.

But that wasn't what caught my attention.

In front of us floated a giant spaceship. Rather, the remains of one.

The hull was battered, pieces ripped away and covered in metal scaffolding. I couldn't tell if it was being repaired or broken down completely.

"Mack..." I looked over at him and undid my harness, kneeling by his side and violating every safety protocol in the book.

His face was pale, bloodless, his eyes stunned and wide.

"Mack, talk to me. What is that?"

"*The Daedalus*. What happened to *The Daedalus*?" he whispered.

And he didn't seem to hear anything I said.

Before I could ask for more, in a shimmer of pale light, a cluster of tiny silver ships, sharp, triangular, and deadly, formed a cloud between us and the wrecked ship.

Their noses all pointed at us, and I braced for weapons fire.

But nothing came.

"Hunter's Darts. But they're not attacking." He blinked, seemed to realize where he was for the first time.

"Zayda, strap back in. This isn't going to be good."

I followed his orders, but they didn't advance, didn't fire.

"Can we go around them?"

Mack eased *The Queen* to port. And the cloud of ships moved with eerie synchronicity, keeping us away from the *Daedalus*.

No matter how we moved, they blocked us.

"We can't go there. I can't go home."

No, he couldn't. But I worried about something else.

"Mack, they knew we were here so fast. How could they know we were coming? They didn't have time to pick us up on sensors and get into formation."

The question snapped him out of his trance. "Wherever my brothers are, they wouldn't still be here. Not with Hunters around. No one would be. It's just an empty ghost now." But he stared long at the ships facing us. "I want answers."

So did I. Brothers, Hunters, I wanted answers to it all.

But first things first.

As one, the swarm of Hunters slowly advanced.

"I don't think they want us here anymore," I whispered.

"I don't want to be here, either." He glanced over. "You think you're pretty sure how that weird engine works?"

"I think so. Maybe. I've seen specs for it."

"Good enough. Let's make sure they can't follow us, then." And, over my protests, he slapped the fold engine on.

For a second, I was pulled in every direction, turned inside out and then back again.

And, suddenly, it stopped.

We were in orbit around Orem Station, Minor blinking above us.

"You were right." Mack caught his breath faster than I did, but even he had a slight tremor to his voice. "Let's not do that again unless it's absolutely necessary." I nodded my agreement. "But I'm glad we're not there anymore. Let's take her in."

As we left *The Queen's* bay, I touched Mack's arm. He froze but didn't pull away.

"We need to go see Granny."

"No. You need to go back to the hive. Tell her the ship's running fine. More than fine."

He was stalling me, but something had to be said.

I touched the back of his neck, where the marks of the mind wipe had faded almost to invisibility. "But there's more to it, and you know it."

Mack's eyes bored into mine, demanding questions I couldn't yet answer. "And of everyone down here we know, Granny seems like she might be able to help."

He snorted, and his fingers wrapped around mine. A little bit of the heavy weight fell away.

"Void knows, she knows everything else. Let's go."

FOR ONCE, Granny seemed surprised to see us. "Everything all right, children?"

"*The Queen* checked out just fine," I said. Mack still looked stunned. For now, I'd talk for both of us. "Interesting little surprise in the engine room."

She smiled. "Thought you'd find that."

"That checked out fine, too. Which turned out to be a good thing."

Her eyebrows rose slightly, but that was the only indication she gave of the significance of what I had said.

"If you've got time, we'd like to talk to you about a few things we found on our trip."

She looked between us, then nodded. "Come on back. Marga, if anybody comes by, tell them I'm out for a bit."

A chorus of children's voices drowned out any response Marga might've made.

As we went down the hallway, I caught a glimpse of the blonde woman we'd rescued that morning from the ghosts. "Is she all right?"

"She will be."

Granny Z stopped at a door and slid open a panel. She entered a code sequence. Nothing happened for long seconds, then Mack pulled me back as the wall before us opened into blackness.

"Sounded like we might need a little more privacy than usual, to talk about your trip." She stepped through into the dark. "Hurry up, children, the door's timed to close quickly."

Instead of going up, to where I had thought most of the living spaces were located, we went down, under the hive, under the decking of the level.

"Where are we?" I wondered, looking around as the narrow stairway suddenly opened up into a room ablaze with light.

"I'm an old dragon, and this is my horde." She sat at a round table, its wood surface gleaming with age.

It wasn't a bad description. Every nook and cranny was filled with countless mementos.

At a glance, I would guess only a small portion had any value other than for the memories, but some of those that did... It was no wonder Granny Z wasn't worried about charging her guests for credits.

"I'll give you a walk through the museum anytime," she said dryly. "But I don't think that's why you wanted to talk."

I looked at Mack, but he seemed lost in thought. I didn't know how, but if the memories were returning, I hoped it was for the best.

"Do you have any way to find and extract a tracker from a person?"

Granny blinked. "That was a little more upfront than I'd expected from you. Any particular reason you're wondering?"

"Yes."

She didn't ask any more questions, just wandered into a corner of the room, rooting through shelves and muttering.

Mack turned to me. "You think there's a tracker."

I guided him to a chair at the table. "Something was obviously done to you. Those ships, those Hunters, they knew you were there the instant we dropped out of warp. Almost like they knew to expect you." I took a deep breath. "I think when your memories were taken, you were tagged, yes."

Anger narrowed his eyes, tightened his jaw. "Get it out."

Granny came back with a scanner several generations newer than what was up at the clinic. I looked at it, then her. "And I'm the one that's not upfront?"

She shrugged and handed it over. "You just don't ask the right questions."

"Let's start with the easy places." I ran the scanner down one arm, then the other. Nothing.

Over the broad plains of his chest, hotly aware that the scanner followed the same path my hands had taken down his skin the night before.

"Turn around, son."

Across the breadth of his shoulders, then... "There it is, the little bastard."

The scanner lit up again as I rechecked. There is was, right under Mack's left shoulder blade.

He stiffened.

"At least we know about it now, right?" I rubbed his shoulder. "Come on, let's see about getting it out."

Mack slid his shirt off and I caught my breath.

Granny's eyes met mine and, for the first time, she looked shocked.

His back was covered in scars, thick and thin ones, straight and curved, until it was a tapestry of pain.

I ran my hand down the skin. The texture was smooth, but the marks told their own story.

How could I not have known?

Then I kicked myself. Easily enough. I'd never seen his back in the light.

"I think we've found the cause of some of those nightmares," I whispered.

Mack shook his head. "Other stuff to deal with first."

Maybe. What I saw couldn't be forgotten. But if he could deal with it, so could I.

"There it is." I found the insertion mark, blended in with the rest of the scars.

I pressed, and could feel it just under the skin. "Doesn't look like we'll have to get too deep into the muscle."

Granny stood up again. "I've got a little bit of numbing agent upstairs, keep it around for the kids."

"Got a knife down here?" I couldn't blame Mack for the carefully controlled rage in his voice. "Use it."

While Granny took a surprisingly long time to find a blade, he wrapped his arm around my waist and rested his forehead on my chest.

I started to speak, but he shook his head. "No. Nothing else until we get this thing out of me. Please, darlin'."

The anger had passed from his voice, leaving only exhaustion.

I stroked his hair in silence until Granny returned. "Here we are, children. Let's do this." She started, then handed me the blade. "Your hands are probably steadier than mine these days. Don't tell anyone, though."

It wasn't deep. I had the tiny dull brass disk out and in my hand almost as soon as I'd made the first cut.

"What do we do with it?"

"Give it to me."

"I have a better idea," Granny said. "I'll be right back." She took the tracker and disappeared back up the stairs.

Mack reached for his shirt.

"Wait for me to bandage it, or we're going to have to go shopping for more shirts for you as well."

But the cut had already started healing.

I thought about that. Thought about what I knew or guessed about him. How deeply and how often the cuts would have to have been made to leave scars like that.

Granny came back smiling wickedly.

"Gave it to the children. Told them to take turns hiding it. I'd give them each fifteen credits if they made sure it was in the worst smelly places they could find."

Her smile faded. "Is this to do with what's happening on Minor?"

Mack and I looked at each other, startled. "What do you know about that?" he asked.

She shook her head. "I know more about the station and that place than probably anybody alive. People are being taken off the streets of my station. Maybe not always good people, but still, my people. People they think no one will miss. Up they go. And, in time, away."

I sat suddenly, knees shaking. The prison was just a convenient place to stash me when I made trouble, was somehow discovered copying over the files. Wasn't it?

What if it was another piece of the puzzle? What if it was the key?

Mack's arms wrapped around my shoulders from behind, and I leaned into him, into his support.

No more choosing. No more lies.

I reached up for his hand, twining my fingers with his, and started the story.

It didn't take long to untangle it all. The mission, the evidence I'd found of collusion between the station's governor and the criminal syndicates. Worse, the large transactions I couldn't trace.

We had a mystery player in the game, and in my bones, I knew it was a deadly opponent.

"Maybe," I finished up. "Maybe the prison is just another part of that. Maybe they need people for some reason, to be moved to Minor, where they can get the labor out of them."

Granny Z nodded. "And when they're not useful even there, the ghosts come."

"When nothing else is left, they're still bodies, still parts." Mack rubbed his head. "That's always going to be useful to someone."

MACK

*G*ranny stood up. "Well, that's put me right off my lunch."

I couldn't even think about food. Not about anything. I hadn't been tired before, but now all I wanted to do was sleep.

Zayda rubbed my shoulder, well away from where she had cut the tracker out of me.

"I'd ask if you're all right, but that'd be pretty stupid right now."

"We've got a big puzzle to figure out, and I'm missing half the pieces. Who knows, maybe a few more nightmares will give us something to work with."

Her face blanched, and I hurried to reassure her. "I'm kidding, but I wouldn't mind some rack time."

"Of course." She stepped away, eyes looking anywhere other than at me.

The hell with that. "I'm too tired to fight, darlin'. Come with me?"

She took my outstretched hand and together we went back to the room above.

I settled in while she blanked the narrow window and then crawled under the covers.

I wrapped my arms around her. I hated myself for saying the words, for being weak. But I had to know.

"You're not leaving?"

"No, I promise." She wrapped around my arm. "Go to sleep."

I've been half joking about trying to get more information from my nightmares, but I wasn't going to turn it down if offered - the next trick would be remembering.

Slowly, I pieced together the fragments from the previous nights, until it started again.

Once more, I was in the room, strapped down. This time, I recognized the men and their questions.

The ghosts from Orem. My brothers and I had called them Hunters. We'd worked with them before, if uneasily. Why were they the enemy now? I tried to look at the room, remember any other details that would help us, but the memory was gray. Either I hadn't seen it, or it hadn't been important.

And then the questions came, and the pain.

That's enough, Mack. Come back.

I slipped into happier dreams.

Hours later I lay with Zayda snuggled in my arms. "What do you think normal people do on days when they just want to stay in bed?"

She giggled. "I wouldn't know. We could watch triD, maybe clean house? I've got it - go shopping!"

I wrinkled my nose. "I've got a better idea." I ran my hand under the edge of her tank, the last of the dreams dissolving in the feel of her silken skin.

Until she swatted my hand. "Not until you're done healing."

Flexing my shoulder didn't bring any pain. "I'm pretty sure I'm fine." I reached for her again, but she squirmed behind me to check.

"You're right. It's closed now. Can't even tell where it was."

There was something wrong in her voice. I pulled her back, searched her face.

"What is it?"

"Someone hurt you, badly."

"Yeah, starting to remember that part. Sort of wish I didn't."

Tears welled in her eyes. "How are you not furious about this?"

I pulled her down to my chest and thought. There was a reason. A good one.

But saying it aloud risked driving her away, breaking whatever fragile bridge we were managing to build.

Still. She had to know.

"Somewhere, locked inside me, there is a raging, howling beast ready to kill anything in my way. And if it gets out, before we know who the target is, I don't know who could end up hurt, or worse."

After a long silence she kissed the side of my neck. "As long as you let me help figure it out, I'm alright with that."

WE SPENT the day doing exactly as she said, lounging around, watching triD, and napping.

In the evening, one of the kids brought two bowls of fragrant rice topped with chopped chunks of curried something or other on the top.

Zayda opened the door dressed only in my shirt.

The kid's eyes were wide, not at the gorgeous sight of her, but about something else entirely.

"Granny says you can eat in your room", he wondered, looking at her. "Nobody gets to eat away from the table. Are you grounded?"

Zayda took the tray from him with a smile. "Maybe for a day or two. But she'll forgive us."

I flicked through channels, mostly celeb heads and old historical seridramas that made no sense to me. "I don't know who these people are, what they did, or why anybody cares."

Zayda poked me. "Somehow, I don't think that's because of the memory loss."

She handed me a bowl, then stared at the screen.

"Wait! Go back one!"

Flicking back, I stared at the screen, then at Zayda's enrapt face. "Really?"

"Shh..." She settled down next to me, transfixed by the story, dinner forgotten. All I saw were a lot of people in what looked like old-fashioned outfits, arguing a lot.

"What is this?" I whispered, and nudged her bowl. "Eat."

"It's the story of the Runaway Concubine, haven't you seen it? Never mind, stupid question. But it's probably the most famous interlude in the entire reign of the previous Emperor." She giggled. "And he's the bad guy."

There was no way out of it. "Alright, catch me up, darlin'."

"A family owes an enormous debt to the Imperial house. They can't pay it, so the father decides to sell off his youngest daughter as a concubine to the Emperor."

I bumped her bowl, and she took another absent-minded bite, watching the man and woman on the screen argue. Or make love. It was a little hard to tell. "So, this is her and the Emperor?" I studied the guy again. "Would have thought he'd have better clothes, even back then."

"No, silly."

My hand froze on the way to my mouth. Chances were good no one had ever called me silly before. If we ever found any of my brothers, I could ask. But for now, I kinda liked it.

"That's the notorious smuggler Bryn Volante. He finds her hiding in the cargo bay of his ship..."

Zayda turned to me, eyes alight. "*The Queen.*"

"Wait, what?"

"His ship was named *The Queen*. She ran away with him, and

the two of them became famous outlaws. Out of his embarrassment, the Emperor sent entire divisions to capture them." She frowned. "Maybe that's more from the films than history, but still, he couldn't have been happy about it."

"How do you know so much about this, anyway?"

"The most romantic story in the history of the Empire? Because, like about a million other little girls, I was named for her."

She poked me with the back end of her chopsticks again. "And that clinches it, why Granny thought my name was so funny."

"Wait a minute. You think our new landlady is a runaway princess?"

"Concubine."

"Whatever. Granny Z is really a pirate queen? Can't be. What happened to the girl and the smuggler?"

"That's it! They disappeared, were never found." She put her bowl down, forgotten in her excitement. "Think about it. It explains everything. An antique ship with an engine like that, her secret room of treasures, the name of the ship...."

"Her comfort level with blades, trackers, and extensive medical gear."

Zayda hit me with a pillow.

"Even if you're right, it doesn't do us any good."

She thought about it. "Probably not." She slumped back against the wall. I took our bowls, tidied the tray, and waited. "I guess I just wanted something to be simple."

"Lots of things are simple."

"Like what?"

"Like this." I kissed her, deep and slow. "You and me, what we have. We're simple." I ran my hand down the side of her face, watching her eyes soften, her mouth grow lax. "Everything else - pirate queens and Hunters and spies and governors - we can deal with it later. I want you now. Simple enough?"

She twined her arms around my neck and leaned into me. "Simple enough."

Last night, when I'd touched her body, a fire consumed me, inflaming me with the need to devour her, to take her and make her mine.

This time, passion smoldered, compelling me to taste every micron of her skin, memorize her response to every caress, discover what made her pupils dilate, her breath come in pants, her heart beat faster.

When I finally pierced her, drawing every shudder and wave that passed through her body into myself, one truth shone through with simple clarity.

Zayda was my home now.

Whatever else emerged from my past, wherever her future took us, everything else was a detail.

THIS TIME, when the dream came, I wasn't in the gray room.

No Hunters loomed over me, no pain waited.

Only rage.

The controls of a small pod twinkled before me, but one red light caught my eye.

Hull breach.

I was losing oxygen, and the jump drive was out.

A quick scan confirmed what I already knew. Not a single planet within range.

Outside the viewscreen, flashes marked where my brothers jumped, one by one, into warp fields far from here. I'd be gone myself, just a flash of bent space, if the emergency launch from the *Daedalus* hadn't thrown me into an asteroid.

I closed my eyes. Even a Wolf would need oxygen eventually. Now there was nothing to do but wait.

With the crunch of metal, I jumped awake, fighting against the harness. The top of the pod peeled back, but, instead of the cold rush of vacuum filling the interior, the pale light of a cargo bay flooded in.

Unstrapping, I rose slowly, my limbs weakened, thoughts sluggish. Had the Doc called us back in? Was the emergency over?

When the Hunters swarmed up the sides to pull me out, I didn't have a chance. I fought, because that's the only thing I had left, springing on the Hunter closest to me, pinning it down, and choking the life out of it.

Mack, please...

A Hunter stood behind me. With a snarl, I reached back, grabbed its wrist and threw it away.

It scrambled to its feet, heading towards me again. Before I could react, a steel beam crashed across my back.

Mack, wake up!

Zayda? What was she doing here?

Something soft wrapped around me, holding me tight. I fought against it, gasping for air, then snapped awake.

Our room was in shambles, the tray dinner had arrived on smashed into pieces.

Zayda stood in the far corner, weight rolled to the balls of her feet, eyes wary. "You back with me?"

I slid down the wall, buried my face in my hands. "It's getting worse, isn't it?"

She sat down next to me and I pulled away. "Did I hurt you?"

"No." But her forearm was reddened. Sickness spread through my gut.

"It's not safe for you to be around me. I need to leave."

She pushed herself into my lap until she straddled me, hands bracketing my face. "I thought we had sorted that out. We're together; the rest of the stuff is complications we deal with. Together."

"I could have hurt you." The image of the Hunter lying before me, his throat crushed by my hands, flashed before me. The body morphed into Zayda's, her bright eyes dull and lifeless. At my hand.

I jerked away, but Zayda, the real Zayda, held me close. "Not happening." She wrapped around me, soft arms bringing me to her neck. "Just rest for a minute, and we'll figure it out."

Her scent, warm and welcoming surrounded me, and I buried my face in her hair. "You sure don't smell like Hunters, darlin'."

She laughed, stroking the back of my head. "Just remember that in your dreams. Give them all a quick sniff test before you try to kill them."

"Void, Zayda. Don't even joke about it. Not this." My arms wrapped around her waist, and all I could think about was how fragile she was. "Maybe we should see a doctor, see if they can figure out what's wrong with me."

"No!"

The panic in her voice came as a surprise.

"Darlin', I could really hurt you next time. I can't," my hands shook, and I pulled her closer. "If I'm fucked up now, how is it going to be if I wake up and I've actually hit you?"

"We'll have to figure it out on our own." She pushed away from me, stared at me long and hard, then closed her eyes. "I know I said no more secrets, but this one isn't mine."

My heart froze. "Whose is it?"

"Yours."

"Not exactly sure how you're keeping my own secrets from me, but I give you permission to tell me." I pulled my hair in exasperation. "Do you even hear how ridiculous that sounds?"

"Mack, this is serious." She took a deep breath, then the words spilled out in one long sound. "You'renotcompletelyhuman."

I blinked. "Try that again? Slower?" But her words started to sink in.

"You know already, don't you?"

I leaned back against the wall, stared at the ceiling. "I suspected something was wrong. I should have needed more oxygen in the shuttle. In the warehouse, I could see you, but you couldn't see me. Little things." I swallowed. "And in my dreams, I know there's something that makes us different. Something the Hunters want.

"How did you find out?"

"When you were in the clinic, I did your scan. You've been altered. Genetically modified more than I've ever seen. Way more than is legal, to be honest."

"And you didn't think to say anything?"

She gave an uneven grin. "I kinda assumed you already knew."

I tapped the side of my head. "Memory gone, remember?"

Zayda pulled away to sit next to me. "I saw the marks. But I've never seen anyone recover as much from a wipe as you have."

"This is recovering?"

"I think the nightmares are your memories coming back, reforming." Her words were hesitant, feeling her way through a theory. "I don't know all of the details, but the wipe fries the neurons of the hippocampus. Usually it erases anything stored in the last few weeks, but nothing stored for longer."

"It did more than that, I can tell you."

She got up, moving around the room as she talked, putting it to rights. I watched her, wondering if she just needed something to do with her hands while thinking things through. "I know that. And I know that doesn't normally happen. We can suppose that the experiences you're reliving are from during the time that should have been wiped."

"And that tells us what?"

"Your enhancements may have saved you. Maybe whatever is changed in your physiology means you store memories differently. Maybe the wipe was enough to disrupt everything, but only temporarily."

I got to my feet in a rush, grabbing her shoulders. "You're saying that everything will come back, just not in nightmares."

"In time, yes, I think so." She turned her face away from mine, the sorrow shadowing her eyes.

"Then what's the problem?" My hands dropped. "It's because of the modifications, isn't it?"

"What?" Zayda shook her head, still refusing to meet my eyes. "I've known about that from the beginning. Don't really care."

"If you don't mind the fact that I'm not entirely human, and probably the result of illegal research, then what's our hiccup, darlin'?"

She spun back, her eyes shone with unfallen tears. "Promise me there's no one else."

"That's easy," I laughed. "There's --"

"No. Stop. Think about it." The force of her words silenced me.

"You didn't just lose a month or two. You lost everything. You don't remember your name. How do you know there's not someone waiting for you out there?"

I folded my arms around her, held her close. Breathed in the sweet smell of her. The smooth touch of her skin that could set me smoldering at any time.

"If there was someone out there, in my past, that meant half of what you do to me, I wouldn't have been compelled to go to some random-seeming coordinates." I cupped her cheek in my hand, willed her to believe me. "I'd have done anything to find her. Since that wasn't the case, she doesn't exist."

Softly, I brushed my lips over hers. "You do. And I'd never forget you, no matter what they did."

The sharp rap at the door made us both jump.

"Come on down, children. We need to talk."

ZAYDA

$\mathcal{A}$s we descended the steps to Granny's parlor, I pushed Mack's revelations from my mind.

No matter what I wanted to believe, he couldn't be certain. There couldn't be anything between us but friendship.

My heart clenched at the thought, but at least we would still have that, right?

People choked the narrow hallway, coming in and out of the hive. I stood on the landing, watching. Mack's hands rested on my shoulders.

"What do you make of it?"

I watched for another moment, spinning my theory. "People come in, excited and curious. Most of them leave, still curious. A fraction are leaving with a different gait to their walk. Excited, maybe, but determined."

"The air reeks with adrenaline," he added. "Probably enough to bottle it."

"That's odd," I mused. "No, not about the adrenaline, I believe you. But everyone who looks like they're heading out on a mission has a bit of red cloth somewhere on their clothes."

"Maybe it's today's fashion? We can ask Gozer when we find a way to check in 'upstairs'."

Maybe. But I would have bet that they didn't have it on them when they came in.

A half-grown kid came and found us in the crowd. "She wants you now." I couldn't help but notice he had a red sash tied around his arm. People fell away from him, making a path for us.

At the door to the treasure lair, he stopped, looked up at a corner of the ceiling.

"Cams," I muttered as the door clicked open, and then I blushed. If there were cams in our bedroom, I'd have words with Granny, childhood hero or not.

But my words died on my lips when we entered her lair. She flipped through an old holo cube, her sharp face softened by sadness. She paused on one, three generations of a family, I'd guess. An older couple stood next to a younger one, all four peering at the infant in the younger woman's arms.

"Live long enough, and you start to think it's time to withdraw from the world. Let the younger folks handle things."

She snapped off the cube with a decisive wave of her hand. "But I know better, don't I?" Her crafty smile slid back into place, and I could almost believe she *was* the legendary pirate queen.

"I need another favor."

"I'm happy to take *The Queen* out any time," Mack answered with a grin.

"I'm sure you would be, son, but not today. Today I need a different type of errand run."

She slid a small, carved, black token across the table. I picked it up, rolled it over in my hand. Something like a modified rectangular prism, chunks carved out of the top so that the line went up and down, up and down all around it.

"What is this?"

"A message. The person at the location I'll give you will know what it means."

When she told us where she wanted us to go, who she wanted us to find, I took a step back.

"You're crazy."

"Probably, but that's not the most polite comment to make."

"Really," Mack looked down at me, "how bad can it be?"

"This is the Lowers. She wants us to go to the Under."

"And that's why I saved this little task for you. I have no doubt that, between the two of you, you can get through to my man." She tapped her fingers on the table and, with a jolt, I recognized my own little tell.

"And once you're down there, you might find out that he has some talents that you want to use yourself."

She handed us two strips of red fabric. "Stick these on somewhere. Those in the know will leave you alone."

"And those that aren't?" Mack grumbled.

"I'm sure you'll teach them manners soon enough."

Once we were on the street, I leaned against the side of the hive.

"What's so bad about the Under?" Mack asked.

I stared at the black abstract form in my hand, musing. "If she sent a code, any sort of message that could be intercepted, someone could break it. Something like this, the meaning could've been decided years ago. It'd be virtually uncrackable."

"Can I see that?"

I handed it to him and he turned it over in the light and then set it down in the palm of his hand, level. "I think it's a chess piece."

"A what?"

"Chess, it's an old game. Doc liked old things, figured it was good for us to learn every strategy game out there. Chess, Go, you name it, she had it on board."

He stopped, and then wrapped his fingers around the piece. "Doc, I remember Doc now."

I wrapped my hand around his fist. "Is that a good thing?"

"Yeah," he let out a long breath. "That's a good thing. Anyhow, let's see where you're so unhappy to go."

To get to the Under, we went back through the bazaar towards the hub of the station. I'd heard of how to get down, but it wasn't the same as firsthand knowledge. I would rather have had a guide. But right now, there were too many games going on, and we didn't know who we could trust. We'd have to figure it out on our own.

Behind a half-torn-down stall at the dingiest part of the bazaar, I stopped by a rusted metal panel. "It should be here."

"How do you know?"

"I don't, exactly." I kept looking for a catch, a sign, anything. "Before I took the assignment, I studied the plans for the station, listened to reports of smugglers that had been captured, tried to learn everything I could. I still don't know how I was caught."

"That can be tomorrow's mystery." Mack rocked each corner of the panel, loosening it until, with a 'pop', it slid free. "We've got our hands full for today."

We started down the narrow stairs, steep enough to almost be classified as a ladder.

"This can't be the only way to get to this place, not as stiff as that entrance was."

I shook my head, knowing that he would be able to see me just fine in the dark.

"It's just the one I know about. An old maintenance passage that connects all the levels, or at least did, once upon a time. I'm sure there's more ways to get down, but I'd expect them to be closely guarded."

"If the Under is as bad as you say, you'd think they'd be more interested in getting out than stopping people from getting in."

I focused on my footing for the next few steps. "It's not that it's bad, just that it's dangerous. But everything I've learned makes me think that they're not that welcoming to strangers. They've made their own world down there, with their own rules."

"Like Jado and Ardelle plan to."

I shivered. "I hope."

Legs aching, we emerged from the stairwell. Mack slid the panel shut behind us as I scouted the area.

We'd left the bazaar in full day shift, here, all was kept in twilight. I looked around, got my bearings, and then wrapped my hand around Mack's and headed off.

The Lower levels mimicked the layout of the Uppers - straight lines, at least the pretense of order, a sense of striving for prosperity, even if you knew you'd fall short.

The Under mirrored all of that. Women dressed in elaborate costumes that called to mind triD dramas, but made of tatters and wiring. Silent children raced out of narrow alleyways, then faded back from us, too quickly for me to make out the strange painted marks on their faces. The streets curled around in maddening spirals, with no addresses, just landmarks to guide us.

As we passed through the district, people looked at us curiously, then looked away, as if deliberately forgetting our intrusion. There was no way to disguise that we were strangers, but no one seemed eager to challenge us. I wondered if their indifference was due to Granny's red tokens, Mack's size, or apathy.

I stopped at the final intersection, reran the directions in my head, and swore under my breath.

"You've got to be kidding me."

Mack followed my gaze and grinned. "Another nightclub?" He cocked his head. "I've some pretty good memories of the last time you took me to one of those."

His thumb brushed my lower lip and, for a moment, I turned to hot liquid thinking of the kiss in the Down Low that had somehow set us on this path together.

And then I shoved the feeling away. "Let's go deliver a game piece."

Calling the place a nightclub might be overstating things. A dingy bar with a few people halfheartedly humping on a makeshift dance floor in the corner would be more accurate.

I pushed through to find a place at the bar. A guy with a reddened, blotchy face, dressed in multiple stained and torn layers, turned and grinned at me.

"Hey, sweetie." His breath was rank. "You look new. You really need to have a guide down here."

He leered towards me until Mack's arm landed casually on the bar between us.

"Thanks for saving me a seat, honey." He dropped a light kiss on the top of my head, then turned his attention to the bartender.

The drunk's eyes widened and he leaned away. "Just offering to be a guide, just being friendly."

"Sure." The approach of the bartender sparked a different thought. "We'll buy you a drink, if you can tell me where to find Mulligan."

"That old kook? What you want with him?"

I turned my back to him, trying to figure out what in this place would be safe to drink.

The bartender stood waiting for our order. Mack rubbed his jaw. "Two of whatever won't kill me." He glanced down at me with one eyebrow raised, as the bartender moved off. "It probably won't, right?"

"True."

"I can take you to him, really. Don't care why you want to go there, he's a loon." The drunk behind me kept muttering, a pleading, wheedling tone woven in his words. "None of my business. But I'd take you."

I nodded to Mack to call the bartender back again.

He reached and filled the barfly's glass from a bottle of a thick greenish liquid. Mack slid the credits over with a slight shudder of revulsion.

We left our drinks on the bar, untouched while we waited for the man.

"Just lemme finish this," he took a quick slurp, then started wiggling away from the bar.

My arm shot out and I grabbed him by the elbow. "If you screw with us…"

"I get it, I get it. He'll beat the crap out of me."

Mack laughed. "You don't get it. I'll let her get to you first."

The man's eyes widened and his head nodded in a quick twitch. "Come on, it's back here."

We made our way through the tables, crowded with people even at this time of day. Though I guessed, if you kept things at a permanent twilight, time of day kind of lost its meaning.

The man stopped at the back of the room, twitched again. "So, even if it's a real easy job, if I do what I said, you're not going to do anything, right?"

I leaned back, thinking. Of course we weren't going to beat him, but what sort of reputation would get us the farthest down here?

I didn't have enough information to guess. "Only if you screw us over," I repeated. "Keep going."

He took three more steps, then rapped on a door frame. The entryway itself was covered in layers of thick cloth that must've been a plush red once, but now was faded and gray with dust.

"Who's there?" A thin surly voice called out.

"Company." The drunk bobbed again, nodded towards the door. "He's in there. I guided you. I'm done." And with that, he scuttled back to the bar.

"Well, I guess we just knock again." Mack's knock held considerably more force.

"What the hell do you want?" came the same surly voice.

"We've got a message for you." I called back.

"Leave it with the barman."

"I don't think you want us to do that." I ran my finger over the sharp edges of the chest piece.

"Someone thought you might want to play a game, that you

might be missing some pieces." Mack paused for a reaction. "But she's got *The Queen*."

I looked up at Mack, startled. He leaned against the wall to wait. "Seemed worth a try. Not sure I'd trust us either, darlin'."

Only silence answered us. I finally turned away, shoulders thrown back in anger, chin high. "We don't even know if this is the right guy. Let's go."

As we stepped away, we heard a flutter of fabric. I fought my grin down. Apparently, Granny wasn't the only one that had cameras waiting outside her lair.

"Wait. Wait. Show me what you have first."

I held the game piece out, but only let the bottom half show. He'd have to let us in to see the details of the top. If I guessed right, that's what would define the meaning of the piece.

"Hold on, hold on. I'll be right there."

Quickly, I handed the token to Mack. We didn't know who was coming, or even how many.

I trusted Granny, or, at least, I mostly trusted Granny. But, on the off-chance that our jittery friend had led us to a trap, an enemy would have a harder time getting the token from Mack than me.

I stretched my shoulders. Not that I was planning to go down easy.

The curtains pushed aside in a cloud of dust. In the shadows, we could see the bent figure of a thin man, not as old as I'd thought from his voice, but someone who had spent far too long out of the light, even for a station dweller.

"Alright, hand it over," he croaked.

"No."

I could feel Mack's surprise, but he said nothing, backing me up.

Granny had said that once we were here, the man in front of us might have something we'd want. But, until we knew more, I couldn't tell what that would be.

"I'm learning how it works down here. Our favor for Granny was to bring the token to you. But I want something from you to complete the delivery."

He laughed, the deep sound echoing in the dark-shrouded corner. "What exactly do you think I have?"

"I don't know. That's why I want to see what's down there."

He looked at us, evaluating, then straightened, suddenly turning into a much younger man than I had first estimated.

"She wouldn't have sent you here if she didn't trust you, come on." Mulligan turned back into the passageway. "Don't fall behind. If she sent a message, something's going down, and soon."

MACK

I followed Zayda through the twists of the maze the man had built.

He didn't have the stink of fear about him. Anticipation, yes, but nothing to the point I worried about an ambush.

Still, I stayed close to Zayda, and kept my ears open.

With a final series of twists, the man stepped out into a large room. Zayda gasped as she stepped into the light and I hurried forward.

The entire room with set up as one massive comm station. Zayda walked from one screen to the next, eyes flickering, mind calculating.

"How far can you reach from here," she asked, wonderingly.

"Far enough," the man said.

She stood over another block of electronics. "And how much can you scramble from here?"

The man grinned broadly. "Enough."

"I think I know why she sent us." She smiled sweetly. "Mack, would you deliver a present to our new friend?"

I handed it over and the man's eyes fixed on the piece. "Well…" he focused on the comm station, our presence already forgotten.

"Wait." Zayda's command cut across the room. "I want to trade for another favor."

"This really isn't the time. You know what this means."

"No, and, to be honest, I don't really care. But you don't run comms like this without wanting information. I know something you don't. Something useful."

He sat down, smirking. "And what do you think that is?"

"Tried to run up to Minor lately?" Zayda's voice was light, but I didn't need to hear the tension in it to know how much she was worried about the explosive situation we'd left behind.

"Not a lot of point." The man shrugged. "Folks go up, they don't come down. The system doesn't send much out, and prisoners don't have access to the comms."

"What if I told you they might not be prisoners anymore and they most certainly do have access?"

Zayda's broad smile matched Mulligan's own as he absorbed the information. "Unless you don't think you can make the connection."

"Don't even try that bullshit." He waved towards another chair. "Let's see if you're telling the truth."

I stood behind Zayda as she sat in the chair, watching his hands fly over the panel.

He shot over a confused look.

"Why would they be calling for her?" he muttered and shook his head. He shot a look our way. "Either of you go by Zayda?"

A smile bloomed on her face. "They're fine. Is there any other message?" She hurried over to his panel.

"Sort of." He brought up a screen of gibberish, then passed his hand over the panel again until it resolved into repeating text. Zayda call home. Zayda call home.

"It's pretty clever algorithm actually. Wouldn't mind meeting whoever set it up."

"Get me a commline up there, and I'll introduce you. I suspect she's a lady after your own heart."

He didn't think for long. "I'll take a trade on that favor. You're on." The man worked for a few more minutes until finally Jado's tech's face appeared.

"Oh, hey!" The bored look was entirely gone now. "You've missed some excitement. Hang on and I'll patch you through to Ardelle. She's been worried sick."

"That makes two of us," Zayda said. She glanced over at Mulligan, who stared at the tech in fascination.

"Actually, can you split me off onto another channel for Ardelle and keep talking to this guy here? He did us a solid favor, might have some stuff for you guys to talk about."

"Why do they keep asking if I can do things," the tech muttered, and suddenly the screen split. Her face on one side, a view of Ardelle and Jado's room behind the Down Low filling the other. From the far corner, Ardelle hurried up.

From his commstation the man separated the two images, sending Ardelle's channel over to where Zayda and I waited, dragging the tech's transmission to another corner.

"We can let them talk shop for a while, I suspect."

Zayda got a good look at Ardelle and reached towards the screen.

"Oh, Void," she breathed. "What happened?

A purple bruise spread over the side of Ardelle's face.

"It could've been worse," she said darkly. "I wasn't the one who could have ended up smothered to death in a box underneath some rich person's dinner. Give me someone I can fight back against, any day."

She shouted over her shoulder. "Babe, they're okay!"

Jado came into the field. A long cut ran down his left cheekbone, but otherwise he looked unscathed.

I met his eyes through the transmission, flicked down to Ardelle's face and raised my eyebrows.

Jado nodded with a tight smirk, eyes flat and cold.

No need to talk about it. I could be pretty damn sure that

whoever had touched Ardelle was even now floating between Minor and the station. In one piece, if the poor bastard had been lucky.

"Everything safe up there, everything solid?"

Ardelle laughed. "As much as it's going to be for a while. Look!" She showed both of her forearms, free of the cuff. "I was so used to wearing it, and now...it's strange, but nice."

"We have access to the parts of the station we need by these." Jado held up a small rectangle and I recognized the control chip from the cuff, cut out from the original housing. He scratched his neck. "Does mean I occasionally forget it."

Ardelle poked him in the side and wrinkled her nose. "All the time," she mouthed.

"But it's a hell of a lot better than having it on all the time. Especially since this version doesn't deal out shocks. Well, not to us." He smiled, and I wondered who was wearing all those extra cuffs now.

"Any trouble with the rest of the population?"

"A couple of the other gangs weren't thrilled about the new order of the world, but they're getting a quick lesson in how to get along with others."

"What about the Hunters?" Zayda asked.

"The what?" Ardelle looked confused.

"The ghosts." I clarified. "That's what they're really called. And they're a lot worse than you realized."

Jado nodded grimly. "We've held off any attempts to board. One shuttle came up, we got the poor idiot off fast enough, then sent it back empty."

"Don't unload anymore shuttles." I hated to say it, I sounded like a monster.

Zayda turned up to me, shock in her eyes, and then she paled, realizing the truth.

"You can't know who's on board," she whispered. "You'll have to assume each shuttle is a trap, at least for now."

"It's a shitty calculation, but you're balancing letting one, maybe two people suffocate against the risk of a shuttle loaded with Hunters on board." I stared at Jado, willing him to understand the severity of this. "If they come to take Minor back, and they get any foothold at all, you won't make it."

Ardelle bit her lip, then her eyes hardened. "We can do that. We fought too hard over the last three days to stake our claim. Getting soft isn't an option."

Someone shouted off screen and Jado slumped, rubbing his face with his hands. "Gotta go do stuff. Being in charge is a pain in the ass."

With a wave and a promise to signal again soon, Zayda cut the connection and turned to Mulligan.

"Even deal?"

"Even." He gave a lopsided grin. "Might even owe you."

Zayda headed for the door. "We're headed back up. Have anything you want us to tell Granny when we get there?"

"Don't worry," he patted the console. "I'll get the message through on my own. Just let her know to expect to hear from me soon."

We climbed the endless stairs back up from the Under, the silence giving me far too much time to think.

If Zayda was right, I just needed to wait a little longer. The memories would return, and I'd know who I was. What was going on. And who I needed to destroy.

I could wait it out on Minor, giving a hand in Jado and Ardelle's war.

But... I looked at Zayda, ascending before me, and my gut decided for my brain.

She might kill me for saying it, but I couldn't leave her alone down here. She still didn't know who had betrayed her, or if it had just been lousy luck that got her sent up to the prison satellite.

As soon as her package arrived, she'd head back to the Agency, back to safety.

Besides, there was something about the messages Granny was sending across the station that told me things would be getting pretty interesting down here soon enough.

When we emerged into the bazaar, she bent, rubbing the backs of her calves. "I should've gotten another pair of shoes."

Probably the sandals she'd picked out to go with the blue dress Gozer had made for her weren't the most practical for tromping up and down maintenance shafts, even if they were kinda pretty.

"We can take care of that easily enough," and I swung her up into my arms.

She stiffened against me. "Mack, put me down." Her voice was so soft I didn't quite believe the words. "Please, put me down."

I set her down gently, the tension in her shoulders cutting away the closeness between us.

"Zayda, what's going on?"

She shook her head, headed back into the bazaar. "Nothing. Nothing's going on at all. I can walk on my own."

I followed, eyes narrowed. I thought we were done with the lies between us, but apparently not.

Seven rows in, a voice called across the hubbub and confusion of the market.

"Missy. Missy, over here!"

Searching across the crowd, I spotted the waving arms of the man we had bought Zayda's sandals from.

"Maybe he'll give you a good deal on a second pair," I tried, but the joke fell flat even to my ears.

We approached his booth to the accompaniment of his beckoning hands. "So glad I found you. Someone's been looking for you today."

I tensed, ready for a fight. That didn't sound good.

"Who?" was Zayda's only response.

"How many people are looking for you?" His brows beetled in confusion, then he shrugged. "The parts man, the scrap guy. He's been gone but heard that you'd been around. Seemed like he wanted to find you soon."

Zayda's face cleared. "Klayson? He's back?"

"Just finished with that job, returned this morning."

Zayda started to step away from the booth, then stilled, turned back. "How did you know he was looking for me?"

The man grinned, then tapped the small piece of red fabric dangling from the cuff of his sleeve. "We all keep an ear out for each other, don't we? Favors are worth more than credit."

Zayda's nodded. "I'll owe you one, then. Thanks."

We hurried through the bazaar until we stood in front of the covered booth where we'd first met Granny.

I rubbed the side of my head. It felt like it had been weeks ago, not just days.

"Klayson?" Zayda's voice rang out. "Are you there?"

"Hey, hey," a large, dark-skinned man came out from the back of the booth. "There's the girl." He leaned over, patted her on the shoulder. "I heard you disappeared, got worried." His eyes narrowed and he grinned. "Seemed too smart to be gone forever. Glad I was right."

"I'm glad you were right, too."

He turned his gaze on me. "Looks like you picked up a new friend."

"Yeah, I did. A good friend."

She smiled, but her eyes were sad. When we got back to Granny's, we were having this out.

"She's a good catch, brother. You keep an eye on her."

"I plan to."

"Klayson," Zayda almost bounced in her impatience.

"I know, I know. I've got it back here. Sorry about that, just glad to see you." He went to the back, rustled around and came forward again with a small black fabric bundle in his hands.

"You were gone, figured you'd be back, but, well, you know how it is. Good job comes along can't turn it down for a maybe."

"I know." Zayda took the bundle, unwrapped it to reveal the chip inside, and turned it over. I assumed she found the marks she searched for because, with a satisfied nod, she wrapped it back up.

Klayson watched the process with approval. "Didn't want to leave it with anybody, figured it was as safe with me out in the Black as anywhere else."

"Thanks again. I hope it wasn't any trouble."

"None for me. And, at the end of the day, I brought in a good haul of interesting pieces, buyers already for half of it. Maybe your little package brought me luck."

She leaned over and kissed his cheek. "Thanks again, but now we've got to go."

Her shoulders slumped as we headed away from the booth. "I can't believe it's over." She spun, eyes large. "I've got to tell Stanton right away."

Unreasoning jealousy stabbed me at the name of the man she'd slipped away in the night to contact.

I knew he was her boss, her friend, but it would take more than just knowing that before I'd be happy to hear about him.

"Sure." But I was eager to get a look at the guy. "Let's find a comm booth."

I couldn't make out much through the crappy connection, so I watched Zayda instead, careful to stay out of the screen's field of vision, and listened in.

The wary, smart operative disappeared when she talked to him, her eagerness to please the man who had saved her from a childhood on the streets shining through.

I didn't like it, it made me nervous. But I couldn't tell if my reaction was logical, or just because I'd decided to hate the guy.

"I'll come in tomorrow." Zayda's voice snapped me out of my thoughts. "Yes, I'm sure I don't want to take the earlier run."

Connection broken, she turned away from the comm booth.

"Everything alright?" That sounded light, disinterested, didn't it?

"Yes." She pushed her hair out of her eyes. "Stanton is just a worry wart. Thinks I should head back right away."

I hated to admit he might be right. But she took my hand and tugged me back to the outer ring of the market. "We need to finish what we started."

"I couldn't agree more." I failed to keep the growl from my throat.

"What?" She blinked, confused. "I'm talking about our favor for Granny. What do you mean?"

Ah. I scrambled for a reply, anything that would explain my gruffness. "Sorry, just hungry." I patted my stomach. "I'm a big guy, can't help it."

She glanced at the lights, judging the time, and then headed the opposite direction.

"We've got time for a quick bite, I'm sure. Then we'll head back to Granny's."

And when we were back, I'd find out what she was keeping from me.

ZAYDA

*E*ven from a row away, I could smell the noodles of the little restaurant Granny had introduced us to the day that we took out *The Queen.*

My hand clenched around the data chip in my pocket. I had it. I finally had it back.

I felt light, like I couldn't stop bouncing. This hadn't been the longest mission I've been on, or the most dangerous, really.

But it was the first time I thought I really might fail.

Finally, I had the files and...

I glanced at Mack and crashed to the ground again.

It was for the best. Once I was out of his way, not distracting him, he'd find the rest of his family, his brothers. And maybe, whoever else was waiting for him. He'd pick up his life without me and all of my chaos.

The dull ache in my chest was something I could live with.

"I don't think we saw the menu, Granny just ordered for us last time," I chattered to fill the silence. "Do you want to try something different, or just stick to what we had last time? Or..."

We turned the corner, and Mack's answer was cut off.

A Hunter stood before us.

I started to back up, turned around.

Another was behind.

A glance down the narrow alley on the left showed only a flash of light on a domed helmet.

"Mack..."

"I know. Sorry, darlin', I think you're still tied up in my mess."

"I don't think it's you they're after." The chip weighed heavy in my jacket, but he wasn't listening to me.

"Stay down if you can. I'll get us out of this."

He shoved me against the cloth side of the booth to the right, the closest thing to cover there was, and launched himself at the Hunter before us to fight them alone.

Not happening.

I waited until the other Hunters' attention seem to be fixed on Mack, then flipped around the corner, scanning up and down to see what booths were here, what they sold, what might be useful.

There was nothing, no weapons, no knives, no... Void, that was a stupid idea, but it was all I had.

I ran up to the man at the junk booth. "Can I have a length of that, and three of those?"

I slammed all the credits I had in my pocket down on the counter.

"Well," the old man started "let me go make you some change. You got someone to help you carry that?"

His movements were maddeningly slow, contrasted with the quick staccato of blows from the fight.

"Keep the change, just give me the things!" He moved slowly towards the items I had picked out and, with a scream of frustration, I grabbed them myself.

This would never work. But it was try, or do nothing.

And doing nothing wasn't an option.

I'd bought a length of cable, frayed at both ends, and small plates of predrilled permasteel, probably for patching hives, joining extensions, hell, I didn't know, didn't care.

I turned away from where Mack fought against the three Hunters. He stood his ground, throwing one after the other off him into the surrounding stalls, but they kept coming back at him.

Without a weapon, I couldn't match their strength or speed.

Hands shaking, I laced the cable through the snap holes of the panels. Up and around, up and around, swearing at my clumsiness.

Take a breath Zayda. You can't help him if you can't get it together.

I glanced over.

The battle wore on. One of the Hunters lay on the ground, leg twitching mechanically, but the other two were still on Mack. Blood ran down his face. He had to be slowing down.

When the last knot was done, I gave my makeshift weapon a test spin and was pleased with how the edges whirled through the air.

"Back off, you bastards!"

I whipped the length of cable over my head, circling it, and the panels flipped out like blades. It picked up speed and I flicked it towards the back of the Hunter closest to me.

As the sharp edges of permasteel cut into its back, it gave off an unearthly squeal, then fell away from Mack.

Good first step.

I gave a flip to the cable to shake the panels loose, and then another tug.

It wasn't coming out.

Dammit.

But at least Mack was only dealing with one opponent now.

Because the Hunter I'd wounded was slowly headed towards me.

Fine. I could work with that.

I looked around for something to wrap the cable around. A support beam, a pylon, something.

And then there was the prick of something cold at my neck.

"Void, you're more trouble than you're worth."

I knew that voice. Had recorded it for hours on the chip hidden in my coat.

"Tell him to stop fighting."

"Like hell I will."

Governor Tyon Valsi. Couldn't see him, but I knew what he looked like, gray hair that somehow always looked greasy. Tall, strong body that had turned to fat years ago. Dressed in the richest of fabrics, yet somehow always looked messy. And the undisputed despot of Orem Station.

The sharp pain dug deeper into my neck.

"Tell him to stop."

"No," I whispered.

He sighed. "I really don't like shouting, it's so exhausting." That didn't seem to stop him when he bellowed past my ear. "Hunters, stop!"

Both the dark figures left standing froze immediately.

Mack crouched, his eyes feral, ready to destroy his enemy.

Valsi's voice dropped to a more conversational tone. "Hey, Wolf, stop, or your girlfriend pays the price."

I stiffened. He knew what Mack was?

My thoughts cut off as Mack's eyes snapped clear.

"Stand down. You might survive this," Valsi jabbed what felt like the tip of a needle gun into me again and I bit my lip to keep from yelping in pain. "But she won't."

Mack's eyes lasered on to mine. Then shifted to the figure standing behind me.

"I will kill you," he growled.

"I don't think you're going to get the chance. Surrender or she dies in front of you."

"Don't do it!" I cried, but it was too late. Mack dropped his arms to his side, his eyes still fixed on mine.

I should've left, I should've taken a shuttle far from the station the moment I had the chip. He would've been safe.

"Hunters, retrieve."

This time, when the two Hunters reached for Mack ,he didn't fight back.

"You're useful after all," the oily voice behind me remarked blandly. "Who knew?"

Then there was a sharp jab at my neck and Mack's frantic howls of protest were all I heard as I slid into darkness.

～

I WOKE up in a blindingly clean white room. Confused, I started to get out of bed and then panicked.

My wrists were strapped to the bed, a drip line attached to my arm. I looked around again, details emerging from the blankness.

Sterile cabinets, a small tray of instruments. Dimmed lights.

I glanced down to see I was in a plain white smock.

Medical bay. I breathed out. I was just in med bay. Soon Mack would come in and tell me how we got out of the fight, and all would be well. My head ached, and when I rolled my head to the side I could feel the pressure of a bandage against the pillow. Must have taken a blow at the end there, but I couldn't remember it.

The door swung open, but it wasn't Mack who stepped through.

"Stanton!" Relief swept through me, then a gnawing worry. "Did you get it, do you have it?"

My throat felt like sandpaper, hoarse and gritty. "How long have I been out?"

"Two days. I asked them to keep you under until I got here."

"Two days?"

"Relax, kiddo. It's all taken care of now." He pulled up a chair, looked at me. The lines on his face deepened, and he shook his head.

"Not sure how this got so tangled up. But it's straightening out in the end."

I sank back into the pillows, ashamed. "I don't know where I messed up. I would've sworn no one was following me, I made no contact with anyone but you. But someone knew enough to call me in."

I thought back to everyone I had encountered in my first stay on Orem. Klayson, it had to be Klayson. Somehow I'd been made, somehow, he knew what was on the chip. I ground my teeth together.

No matter. Now that I had returned to the arms of the Agency, it'd be easy enough to run his record, figure out how he had been turned

Stanton's voice cut through my thoughts like a laser.

"I thought I trained you to think better than that, kiddo. Nobody on Orem set you up. *I* told the governor what you'd found."

I jolted against the restraints. "What?"

"The whole thing was a bit of a fishing trip." He leaned back in the chair, long legs stretched before him.

I couldn't turn away from his face, this couldn't be Stanton. This was a nightmare, a concussion, a reaction to the drugs, but not Stanton.

But Stanton or not, he continued on.

"There were concerns that Valsi had gotten lax with his security. A mutual friend asked me to send someone over, see how much could be dug up."

He nodded towards me. "So, I did. Man, Valsi really had gotten sloppy. No matter. We've got the chip now, we'll know what to look for, what to tighten up." He patted my shoulder. "You did a good job."

The ache in my head blurred my thoughts. "This was just some kind of security test? The files I found were just plants? Then why was I arrested?"

"That was a colossal screw-up."

I relaxed a fraction. It wasn't my job to question missions. If

Stanton had sent me to scout something, there had to be a good reason.

"I told that idiot to wait, let me come pick it up, but he had to panic and snatch you."

He told that idiot… Stanton was working with Valsi?

"And then we realized you didn't have the chip on you."

"But I was bringing it to you, before I got spooked," I whispered. "If you had told me this was a security exercise, I would have just handed the chip to you."

"Like I said, he panicked. By the time I knew anything about it, you were already up on Minor and we had no idea where the files were, or how much was on them." Stanton's warm voice had turned cold, dripped with derision. "Valsi thinks he's smart, decided he could play the game. Since you were already in his little prison, he'd get one of his informants to cozy up to you, see if you'd spill."

"But you had to get mixed up with that animal." His nose wrinkled. "And it all went to hell."

"You know about Mack?" I whispered.

"Of course we do. Another failed project that I'll need to dispose of." He stood up, brushed off the front of his pants.

My mind reeled. "But why not just let me come in, bring you the chip myself?"

Stanton headed to the door. "You'd have been logged entering the Agency. No, you needed to disappear in the field."

The door opened to his touch. "And now you will."

MACK

*T*hey killed her.

Even in the worst of my nightmares the torturers had failed to inflict this much pain.

This room was white, not gray, but the doctors in their masks and their Hunter guards were all the same.

But I didn't care.

For two days, all I saw were Zayda's eyes widening with shock as the needle gun fired against her throat in the bazaar. Her fragile body collapsing to the deck. The spill of hair falling over her face.

Over and over, I watched her perish in my mind, as they cut and burned and prodded me, not realizing I'd already died.

"And here's another fiasco."

The voice taunted me with its familiarity. I knew it from somewhere.

"All we wanted you to do was go find the rest of your miserable pack." A tall, thin man, face lined with age, paced into the room. He didn't smell like a doctor. Didn't smell like much of anything. "But no, you led us straight back to your den. *The Daedalus.* Obviously, we've already acquired that."

A growl broke through my chest as I placed the voice from the comm booth. Stanton. Zayda's trainer. Her savior.

Her betrayer.

He wandered to the front of the tilted slab I was strapped to, and I lunged at him, the thick restraints cutting into my forearms.

"You killed her!"

"Who, Zayda?" He raised one elegantly suited shoulder with indifference.

"You weren't ever supposed to cross paths. Another one of Valsi's screw-ups. I'll be reporting him to the Compound, suggesting a replacement is found. Clearly, he's no longer capable of being even nominally in control of this sector of operations."

"The Hunters, the kidnappings... this is an Imperial operation?"

Stanton smirked. "Doctor Lyall didn't build you creatures for smarts, did she? The Empire can't handle its affairs next to its own heart, much less out here. Besides, the pay is lousy."

I could only stare in disbelief. Zayda had believed in this man, in the job he'd recruited her for. And it had all been based on deception.

"By the way, she's not dead. At least, not yet. Valsi thinks she'll be useful for keeping you in line. I don't really care."

He circled around the table again, his cold eyes absorbing everything, discarding information deemed useless.

"I think your entire breed should be eradicated as uncontrollable, a futile experiment. You're breed isn't a valid research path." He smiled, a mouth full of knives and lies. "And I have just the way to demonstrate it to the others at the Compound."

Not dead yet.

"She's not dead," I whispered to myself.

"Not yet, but I expect she will be soon."

Silently, I strained against the restraints until he passed in front of me again.

I lunged at him, the sudden force breaking my left arm free.

"You first."

My fingers wrapped around his throat, but he just raised one hand and snapped his fingers.

Out of the shadow of the doorway a Hunter fired a small gun twice, the impact against my chest no more than an irritating pinch.

Stanton didn't fight, didn't claw at my hand, just stared calmly as the Hunter fired three more darts.

Waiting.

The first wave of vertigo hit, and my grip slipped.

Stanton stepped away, straightened his collar.

"Thank you. I've won a small bet with Valsi. All of his security is weak."

"What is this?" I slumped back against the table.

A new team of doctors, faces covered with surgical masks, swarmed the room.

"We've made some interesting discoveries from your other "brothers" in the last few weeks. It turns out it's not that difficult to suppress your higher reasoning, such as it is, and enhance your more bestial traits."

The room swam before me, the white uniformed doctors melting in and out of the walls.

"What did you do to them?" I thought I said the words, but everything was fuzzy. It might have only been in my mind, but Stanton answered.

"They refused to cooperate. The General decided it would be an amusing punishment to make them fight each other. Make the survivors watch."

My stomach clenched, and not only from the drug raging in my veins. Flickers of memory, faces of men I would kill for. Had killed for. Now treated like puppets.

"They wouldn't do it, would they?" I ground out the words. It wasn't a really question. I knew better.

"Annoyingly, they killed themselves, rather than fight." His teeth flashed, and, for the first time, the smile reached his eyes. I wished it hadn't.

"That's why I had them double your dose."

I sank back, eyes closed. "There's no one here for me to fight. Unless you're volunteering."

His voice faded away as I fell under the dark waves of the drug. "There's always Zayda."

ZAYDA

ake up, girl.
The voice followed me into my exhausted sleep. Every fiber of my being was worn out, shredded, done.

"I didn't take you for a quitter, and these vents are less comfortable than I remember."

I struggled back to the surface, but saw no one else in the room.

"Up here."

In the tiny ceiling vent, I could see something flickering. No, someone holding something dark against the light mesh.

"Granny?"

"Hold still, child. A sheath would have been better, but then you'd have to deal with it on your end."

While my mind wrapped around her words, a slim shape appeared from the grills of the vent, and slowly I could make out a knife as it slid between the bars. It hovered in the air, then, finally, I could just make out the glistening fine thread that held it suspended.

Unfortunately, it was being lowered a meter past my feet.

"Um, Granny?"

"I'm not blind. Hold on." Unhurriedly ,she began to swing the blade towards me. The sharp edge captivated my gaze as it approached, then retreated, then swung again closer.

"There we go."

With an almost inaudible plop, the blade flew free at the height of its arc, landing on the fabric of my thin gown.

"You can pull it the rest of the way with the fabric."

I had just enough flex in my right arm to reach the hem of my gown. I gathered it one pinch at a time until, slowly, the thin covering carried the knife towards the curve of my hip.

"Almost done, there you go." Her words were reassuring, if I didn't think about the rest of the situation.

"What are you doing here," I whispered, my eyes fixed as the blade moved closer and closer to my hand.

"Busting you out. What did you think?"

Finally, the knife tumbled down my hip and, by forcing my hand through the restraint as far as I could, I finally gripped the blade.

Carefully I turned it in my hand until, bending my wrist back on itself, the blade reached the edge of the restraint. I worked at the bond, sawing through one fiber at a time.

My focus was so intense I didn't hear her until she spoke my name.

"Zayda," she repeated. "Would you mind trying to work the blade further over on the side of your arm?"

I paused, blinked. "What?"

"That knife is one of my sharpest. I'd rather you didn't bleed out mid-rescue."

I looked again, this time focusing past the restraint to the shallow cuts I'd already made on the inside of my wrist. That made sense.

I'd nearly worked all the way through the strap holding my right arm down when, with a quiet click, the door unlatched.

Granny scooted out of sight down the vent faster than I'd have believed from someone her age. Quickly, I twisted as far as I could to the left, sliding the knife under the edge of my right hip, hoping that the trailing length of the thread would be unnoticed.

When Stanton entered, the flare of emotion in my chest made me clench my jaw. His betrayal of me, of the Agency I thought we both believed in, knocked the foundations of my world. As much as I'd craved his approval before, I hated him now.

Still, a small part of me insisted this was all a terrible mistake. That he'd save me, like he had when I was a child.

But the coldness in his expression when his gaze swept over my body killed that hope for all time.

"I've been recalled to the Compound, so we won't be seeing each other again."

"The where?" my mind whirled, trying to remember an installation with that name. "Back to the Agency?"

"You really are turning out to be a disappointment. Do try to keep up with the situation." He shook his head and glanced at his chrono.

My finger brushed against the edge of the knife under my hip.

He was within reach.

At this point, I was quite familiar with the sharpness of the blade.

It would be so easy. One quick slash across his throat.

Either he didn't see the heat in my eyes, or he didn't care.

"I know you're worried about your new pet. So, I've arranged for you to see him one more time."

My hand moved away from the knife. Mack was alive, and here. I could wait.

"Unfortunately, my shuttle leaves too soon for me to stay and watch your reunion."

Despite everything, the words spilled from me. "All of these years, all of the time you spent training me. None of it mattered?"

He halted by the door. "It mattered. You were useful for longer than expected. But, in the end, you were a disposable tool. Why do you think I recruit from the Lowers?" He laughed, that easy sound I'd come to treasure, and it ripped a hole in me. "Not for any sense of redeeming society's dregs. You came from nothing. No one will miss you."

The door closed behind him and I shook silently in the bed. I could scream for hours and still not empty out the well of hurt. And it wouldn't do any good, anyway.

I got back to work.

"It's all lies," I whispered.

"Not everything, child. Not your man. I saw how you looked at each other. There's no other truth that matters."

I examined the right restraint. Almost there. With grim determination, I started sawing at it again.

"You were taken before I had control of the station back yet, I'm sorry. We're about ready to move in. Once you're free, we'll get you out of here."

"No. Not without Mack."

"Child," the voice was soft now. "I think it's too late for him."

'You wouldn't have left Bryn."

The rustling in the vent stopped. "I figured you were smart. You're very, very smart."

"Since I'm stuck here for a bit, why don't you tell me a story, Granny. I'll owe you a favor, later."

She chuckled, and I heard her get comfortable, or as comfortable as one could in an air shaft.

"Bryn and I had a life of adventure. We never wanted to settle down. He would have given me the universe. And he was my entire universe."

"What changed?"

"We had a baby. A little girl. And suddenly, we wanted more." She paused, and I stopped working, waiting for her next words.

"A home. We started building one. We'd never really kept track of what we'd made off with. The credits were never the point. It was the game, the excitement. Being together. There was enough. More than enough."

"Where did you go?"

"Right here, where else?"

"You moved to the station?" With a snap, the final section of the right restraint came free. I flexed my hand and rolled to the left as far as I could, but the locked clasp defeated me.

"No, we built it."

With a sigh, I started cutting again, then her words caught up to me. "You built Orem Station?"

"It never was meant to be Orem. Aurum. Gold. Our pot of gold at the end of the rainbow." She laughed, softly. "He liked puns, that man."

"In the beginning, it was all a bit like the Under. A fantastic haven for all comers. In time, merchants came, and then buyers, until it sorted itself out into Levels, classes. Just like a damn Cilurnum station. But people did what they wanted, stayed within our admittedly loose guidelines, and we were happy."

The left restraint was easier to demolish, and, happily, with fewer cuts on my arm. I started on my ankles.

"What happened?"

"When Sallia grew up, she fell in love. He wouldn't have been my choice for her. But that would have been hypocritical, wouldn't it? A rich man, but not an honest pirate. Just a merchant. Maybe when we told her stories she only heard about the risk, the dangers, but I wished she'd had more love for adventure."

"In time, Bryn and I decided to share more of the responsibility with them, and when Tyon was born, you could have powered the station with our happiness."

The family in the holocube. They had looked happy, sweet for a family of pirates and smugglers and...

"Wait. Tyon?" The knife almost dropped from my hand and I scrambled to catch it before it fell to the deck, out of reach. "Tyon Valsi, the governor, is your grandson?"

"I know. I don't know how he turned out to be such a bastard. Every time I tried to suggest that he make different friends, was going down the wrong path, he threw my past in my face."

There wasn't anything to say to that.

"And when Bryn died... most of me did as well. I ceded control entirely, returned to the first hive Bryn and I had built while we were working on the rest of the station. Let life roll on without me."

She fell silent. I didn't ask anything else, just imagined what it would be like to have that sort of life, the risk of loving someone so much that when they died, part of you did, too.

Like I loved Mack.

"Granny, you said you had people on the way, right?" The left ankle finally came loose. One to go.

"They'll storm the compound as soon as we're clear." She sighed. "Poor little bastard doesn't even know he's lost control yet. I expect he'll throw a tantrum when he does."

It might have been a stupid decision, but it was the only one I could live with. "You should go, now. Start the assault."

"Girl." She paused. "Zayda. You're still trapped."

"So's Mack." I looked up towards the vent, wishing I could see more than shadow, and forced a smile. "Thanks for the knife."

She snorted. "I'll expect it back when we come and get you."

"Come get us both."

The rustling faded away, and I focused on getting free from the last strap.

This time, I didn't hear the door when it opened.

Valsi strutted in, looked at my free arms, and shrugged. "It's not going to make a difference."

Two uniformed guards followed, dragging Mack between them, covered in blood. They threw him into the far corner, and he lay still, limp.

My hands flew to my mouth to stifle the scream.

"Bastard cost me five of my best men," Valsi sneered. "I don't think having your arms free is going to make much of a difference when he comes back around."

The guards backed out of the room, and, despite his brave words, Valsi hurried after them.

With a click, the door locked.

I clawed at the last restraint holding my ankle down, unable to take my eyes off Mack.

I couldn't see him breathing.

There was so much blood.

When the knife finally cut through the strap, I tumbled off the bed with a sob.

"Mack, wake up, please, babe." I crawled to him, legs too shaky to support me, and pulled his head into my lap.

He didn't respond. This wasn't like his nightmares, when he tossed and turned, fighting the ghosts of his past.

He was so still.

I cut the hem of my gown, tried to mop the blood from his face and shoulders. Plenty of new cuts decorated his back, but I had the sense more blood had been spilled than his alone.

Good.

I held him, rocking, trying to come up with a plan, when he coughed.

"Mack, thank the Dark...."

His golden eyes blazed, but with no recognition, no under-standing.

I reached out to smooth his cheek, and he scrambled back, face twisted into a snarl.

Mack, my Mack, was gone.

MACK

 *K*ill them all.

The fire in my blood demanded it, the insatiable urge for battle. I swept the room, searching for enemies, but there was no one to fight.

A howl of frustration broke from my chest and a small figure skittered away. The scent wasn't of them. Different, strange.

Female.

I prowled closer, the pulse at her throat drawing me in.

She pressed against the wall, making noises that made no sense. The sounds enticed me, made me crave more.

One small ankle stuck out and I ran my face down the length of her shin.

Blood. The female had blood on her and the rage spiked again.

Her hands brushed my shoulders lightly and, instead of the skin-crawling revulsion I had felt near the enemies in the other room, I yearned for more.

I wrapped an arm around her waist and pulled her closer, underneath me where I crouched, surrounding her, covering her.

Fear glazed her scent, but her fragrance wrapped around me cushioned the knife edge that tore at my mind.

197

I buried my face in her neck, then moved down her body, the urgency to be near her spurring me on.

The thin fabric stopped at her upper thigh. I pushed it out of the way and then jumped in surprise when she smacked my arm.

No.

I understood the word. But I didn't like it.

I reached for her again, and she slapped my arm, harder this time. Not enough to do damage, but her displeasure was explicit.

My eyes narrowed, but, despite my growl, she pulled my shoulders until her face was level with mine, hands on either side of my face.

Stay with me, Mack. Come back to me.

Just sounds, but I read the meaning in her scent, her touch.

Snarling, I sat back, twisted until we were in the corner of the room, holding her in my lap, caged by my arms.

She talked, soft voice like calming strokes, matching the soothing patterns she caressed on my shoulders.

Breathing deeply of her scent again, I settled down to rest, and waited for the enemy.

ZAYDA

*H*is skin burned under my hands.

I kept talking, chattering about nonsense, fighting to keep the anger and tears from my voice.

Mack's lids drifted half-closed, but the tightness of his arms around me put to rest any thought I had that he might be going to sleep.

"Once we're out of here, we should take a vacation. Go find one of those garden domes. I've always wanted to do that. I get the feeling you probably never have or maybe you have and don't remember. Either way, that would be nice."

With every word, with every touch, his breathing evened.

Whatever they had done to him, it would wear off eventually. It had to.

So, the plan was simple.

Keep talking until I had Mack back with me. Wait for Granny to find us. Figure it out from there.

"Maybe we can find a nice planet, something with breathable air outside of the domes. It'd be fun to do some exploring, wouldn't it, honey."

I traced the hard planes of his face, and he nuzzled into my hand, as desperate for my touch as I was for his.

"Or maybe we'll just steal *The Queen* from Granny, zipping off and becoming this generation's hero pirates-"

The door splintered open and I screamed.

Three men spilled into the room, their faces covered with helmets, not the opaque black of Hunters, just men trying to kill us.

Somehow that wasn't any more comforting.

Before the last echo of the scream had left my throat, Mack rolled, tucking me into him, until we were behind the bed frame.

He snarled and, with a twitch of his hand, the first guard fell.

Another twitch, and I saw that Mack had grabbed Granny's knife, having retrieved it with a precise tug of the thin thread.

Before the first hit the floor, the other two guards followed, each jetting blood from the surgically placed wounds at their throat.

"Stay here," he rumbled, and despite having seen three men killed in front of me, my heart leapt at his return to speech.

He moved to the door, or where the door used to be, and searched the bodies for weapons.

Shots and screams resounded down the corridor.

The attack had begun. But would Granny find us before the rest of the guards?

Mack paced the room, his fragile grip on calm shattered.

Footsteps pounded towards us, and he spun and fired.

Oh Void, let that have been a guard.

"Mack, can you come back and stay with me?" I hated the quiver in my voice, but maybe this was one of the times that excused it.

His gaze tracked the movement outside, and I could see the urge to join the battle, unleash the rage that simmered under his skin.

"Please, Mack. I'm frightened."

Instantly he returned to my side. "Hold this." A blaster landed in my lap, and, with a wrench and the scream of bending metal, he tore the bed I'd been confined to from the floor, laying it on its side before us to form a shield.

"Better."

Attention still fixed on the door, he settled beside me, one hand possessively on my leg. I wrapped my fingers through his, wishing I had the strength to keep him here. Because, out on the battlefield, it wouldn't matter who he met - Valsi's men or Granny's. Right now, until the drug wore off, they were all the enemy.

"Out there," I started, reaching for words as carefully as stepping across a thin bridge, waiting for it to collapse under me. "There are people who are your friends. My friends. They're coming to help us."

He didn't give any indication that my words made an impact, but I forged ahead.

"I know you don't know who they are, but do you trust me?"

The slightest of nods, and the permisteel band around my chest loosened just a bit.

"If someone comes in, can you wait, just a minute, for me to see if they're a friend?"

"No."

Well, he was listening at least.

"Why not?"

"Risky."

"Can we find a way for me to see, without being exposed?"

His head tilted, considering. Then, with a leap, he ripped off the cabinet doors, angling one by the entrance to the room, the other by our makeshift fort.

"There."

The reflection of the doorframe wasn't flawless, but it was a good compromise.

"Perfect." I kissed his cheek, but he turned, mouth falling on mine, his hand pulling me so close into his lap that the hard length of him ground into me.

I wanted Mack back, but this was not the time. Gasping, I pushed away.

"Not now, we could have an audience at any moment."

He frowned, and I braced to remind him again. But he sat back, clearly thinking. "You don't like an audience."

"No, babe, I don't. Thank you for remembering."

The sounds of battle outside our room slowly died down. All we could do was wait. The time stretched out until I was ready to snap.

"Just a quick peek down the hall," I argued.

He shook his head. "I can still hear them."

I couldn't, but I didn't have his enhancements.

"You have to stay here, stay safe."

I knew he'd keep me safe. But could I protect him?

After an interminable silence, once again footsteps strode down our hall. Not the heavy boots of guards. Mack stilled at my touch and I studied our makeshift mirrors, waiting to see who would be revealed. But his voice gave it away.

"Void, I hope that animal tore you to pieces, you bitch. Stanton said it would all be handled, but now it's all falling apart."

Valsi staggered into the room. In the watery reflection, I could see his clothes were torn, hair stood on all ends around his face. As he spun through the room, he stumbled over the body of one of his guards.

"Dammit," he whimpered. "There's nothing left, I can't even get back to the Compound."

The Compound. Stanton had mentioned that. Which meant Valsi had information I wanted.

I stretched to reach Mack's ear, barely moving my lips, trusting he'd be able to hear me. But would he do as I asked? That would be another story.

"Can you wound him? Stop him without killing?"

Tucked against Mack's side, I couldn't see him roll his eyes, but felt the snort echo in his chest.

Just then, Valsi must have caught a glimpse of our reflections. He spun towards the overturned bed, reaching for a weapon, but it didn't matter.

Mack vaulted over the frame, swung him over his shoulders and then threw him against the wall, where he slid down to lie with the corpses of his guards.

I crept out from the hiding place to stand behind Mack.

Valsi still breathed, but he wasn't going anywhere. Mack's breathing was ragged, his eyes fixed on the limp body. "Should've killed him."

I remembered his grip on my neck, the sharp sting of the needle.

"I know. But we might need him. And we owe Granny a favor."

I tied Valsi up under Mack's watchful gaze and we returned to our corner behind the screen of the bed.

My nerves frayed in the silence. Despite Valsi's panic, what if Granny Z didn't win? Would someone come looking for the governor, find us? I glanced at Mack.

For the sake of everyone involved, I hoped not.

"Children? You still in there?"

I shot to my feet ,despite Mack's grip on my arm.

"They're friends. I promise." He stepped in front of me.

The recent wounds on his back had already started healing, but still, I was careful where I put my hands.

"Trust me."

First to appear were a man and woman, faces half covered with red cloth, their eyes grim as they scanned the carnage inside. They stepped aside to let her through.

Granny had changed her long skirts for heavy boots and pants full of pockets, a bandolier of knives crossed over her chest and her gray hair braided into a crown around her head.

"Told you I'd come back."

Then she saw Valsi on the floor, struggling against his bonds. Emotion flickered on her face, and then doors of steel closed over her face.

"Well. Answers that question. Think your friends up on Minor would like a new farmhand?"

Before we could answer, Valsi rolled over, one of the blasters from the dead guards clenched in his bound hands, aimed straight at his grandmother's chest.

"You old bitch. You never let me-"

Mack's shot cut off the rest of his tirade.

I stood closer to Mack, desperately hoping her soldiers would understand he didn't have a choice.

No one spoke.

Though Granny's eyes were bright with unshed tears, her voice was hard, resigned.

"Maybe it's for the best." She turned to address one of the men behind her. "You! Get in here. One of our own could use a little more covering."

I glanced down at the soiled and torn scrap of gown that remained on me, and winced.

A tall man came into the room, stripping off a coat that on me would be nearly a dress. "Here you are, ma'am." He reached to hand it to me and Mack growled, raising his weapon.

"No!" I slid in front of Mack, waiting for him to see me, only me.

Showing great intelligence, the man froze. Granny took the coat from the man's hand and pushed him behind her.

"I'm just going to put this on the floor here."

I darted out, slipped it on, grateful to have my behind covered.

Mack slowly lowered the weapon as I returned to his side.

"He's not usually this bad. They did something to him."

Granny shook her head. "I know. It's been a hard few days for all of us." Her eyes drifted to Valsi's body, and I thought about that happy family in the holo. "We'll see you out there. I've got a station to put back together."

Soon enough, her team left the room. "Are they gone?" I asked "Are you alright?"

Mack nodded. "No one's left." He took a shuddering breath. "I've got a hold of it, for now at least."

"Then let's go."

I twined my fingers with his and we walked out into a new world, both for the station and for us.

MACK

The four of us sat in a deserted open square, steaming bowls of noodles balanced precariously on a rickety table someone had set up and abandoned long ago.

Jado and Ardelle had come down on the first shuttle available after Granny's comm man sent a message up, leaving Minor for Seig to deal with for the day.

There had been hugs all around, and I only growled a little bit when Jado touched Zayda.

Zayda raised an eyebrow, and I rubbed the back of my neck.

"Sorry, still a little messed up."

That was an understatement. The fire still burned in my veins, but, so far, I'd kept a handle on it. I still didn't like Zayda to be further than I could reach. She'd drawn the line at the privacy booth.

But I hadn't tried to kill anyone today, hadn't gotten entirely lost in the madness, and, in theory, that was progress.

I remembered people at least. Granny, Jado, Ardelle, even the blonde woman we'd rescued from the Hunters. Mixed in were memories from before, some faces, a few names from the past.

Slowly it was all returning.

And when it was back?

The future still gaped black and unknown before me.

"So, all this time you were some sort of spy?" Ardelle shook her head.

"I thought I was." Sadness crossed Zayda's face, and I squeezed her hand, wrapped in thoughts she wouldn't approve of.

Killing Stanton wouldn't be because of the drug.

"But I have a mission of my own now." She rubbed her shoulder against mine.

Jado and Ardelle went on about their plans for the station. Well, Ardelle talked, and Jado nodded.

Zayda would tell me anything I needed to know later. Now, something hung in the air, just out of range.

Something dangerous.

"...regular shuttles. Granny asked if we'd give her a hand. There may be a bit of reshuffling, but I think most people won't care who's in charge, now that the decks are safe again at night."

I pushed away from the table, noodles forgotten, focused on a couple entering the park. A dark-haired man and a woman with copper skin. He towered over her, and something in his movements made my fingers reach for a weapon.

Jado came beside me. "Trouble?"

"I don't know."

"Killian?" The man's face danced on the edge of memory, but nothing solid came. "They said one of us was here, but I didn't believe them."

"Sorry, you've got the wrong guy."

He stepped towards us, towards Zayda, and I fell into a defensive position. The stranger halted, took a posture that mirrored mine.

Jado studied the stranger, then me, and back again. "Mack, you sure you don't know this man?"

The gentle touch at the small of my back sparked a growl of frustration. "Zayda, stay behind me."

"Mack, I want to talk to the woman. And I can't do it through you."

She stepped to my side, and I was blackly amused to see the same exasperation on the stranger's face when his companion did the same.

"Davien, leave it alone. Seriously." The woman ran her hand through her short, chopped hair, rolling her eyes. "I'm Kara. I get the feeling we need to have a long talk."

Zayda contemplated her and the man without answering for long moments, fingers tapping. "What do you think we should discuss?"

"*The Daedalus.*"

THE END

LETTER FROM ELIN

Dear Reader,

Does it make me a bad person that I think feral Mack is adorable? Because I totally do.

I promise one of these days I'll write some adventures with Granny Z and her pirate king - because you just know they got up to all sorts of mischief and sexy times!

In *Freed*, things take a darker turn. Ronan has been trapped at Base with the Hunters for too long. He's seen things. Done things. But maybe, just maybe, the touch of the prisoner he's just rescued can bring him back from the edge of madness.

And the pieces of the mystery of the *Daedelus* begin to come together!

Click on over now!

XOXO,

Elin

PREVIEW OF FREED: BOOK FOUR OF THE STAR BREED

onan

Two Hunters on patrol passed below me.

My lip twisted in a snarl but Erich shrugged as if to ask 'what did I expect?'

He was right. Hunters weren't the brightest things out there, but either they or their handler had some basic survival instincts.

I'd been picking off every lone straggler I found on the ship for… well, not sure how long now. But someone finally wised up, had them running patrols in pairs.

Fine.

Two at once would just make the overall job faster.

I dropped from the shadowed beam over the passage to the lower cargo bay, my feet hitting the deck plates with only a whisper of a sound.

Erich was right by me, his moves silent as always.

I tightened my grip on the long, narrow wicked blade in my

hand and plunged it between the shoulder blades of the Hunter to the left.

The first one fell with an earsplitting screech as I severed the cords and cables that passed for a spine.

Unfortunately, that gave its companion plenty of warning.

Without a glance down for its companion it swung at me. I rolled back, swearing. Darkness, I wished I'd found a blaster, a needle gun, something on the damn ship.

But in all the time I'd spent killing the bastards, I hadn't found any real weapons. That was alright. I kinda liked ripping them apart, the way they'd done to us.

When I stood up from the wreckage I checked over the bodies again, tearing open their plated armor, exposing the tangle of . flesh and wiring below.

Still nothing I could use.

I straightened, wincing a little.

Not smart, but excellent combat drones. I'd give them that. I took a deep breath, and stopped myself at the stab of pain at my side.

Bastard had cracked a couple of ribs. And from the dull ache radiating through my arm probably did a number on my shoulder, too.

Erich fell into step with me as I headed back towards my hideout. "You can't keep doing this, Ronan, not without medical care, not on those crappy rations."

I grunted, but couldn't argue, just rubbed the long, raw scar across my throat.

I healed fast, we all did. But even Wolves needed some down time between missions. Here it was just one long fight.

"At least stop by their lab, see if there's anything you recognize, can scavenge."

Erich was right. Erich was always right. It was one of his annoying traits these days.

I changed directions, loping through the empty halls. Hunters had their routines, and I had them mostly mapped out by now. I'd caught the last two on their way to a part of the ship I hadn't been able to gain access to. Yet.

Which meant the lab was unguarded.

I stopped at the door, bracing to go in.

Not much bothered me, certainly not anymore, but this room of people strapped to beds, sliced and poked and prodded, shook something at my core.

I looked at each still form as I walked through, teeth bared at the stink of sweat and pain and adrenaline.

"You should help them." Erich stood at the foot of a bed holding a middle aged man, right arm removed at the shoulder. Drip lines of Void knew what ran into his chest.

"Not a doctor," I muttered. "I'd probably kill them just getting them out." And there was nowhere to take them. My fist clenched around the knife handle. The only thing I could give them was a quick end. Maybe that would be enough, but I didn't know. Couldn't judge.

Only six in the beds now. The remaining two lay empty, ready for new patients.

I rummaged through the cabinets, looking for anything that would ease either my pain or theirs, but it was all labeled with strings of numbers. No telling toxin from treatment.

A tube of wound sealant was the only useful find. Grabbing it, I turned, more than ready to get out of the creep show.

And my gaze was riveted by a wide pair of green eyes, staring at me from a cage pushed to the back of the room.

A woman, long pale hair tangled and matted, crouched inside.

"Help me."

Nadira

ELIN WYN

ONCE UPON A TIME A TALL, bearded wild man with a tangle of
dark hair and jagged tattoos spiraling over half his chest would
have scared me.

Once upon a time, back in my safe little world at the capitol, I
would have crossed to another glide, stayed out of his way, never
met his eyes.

Once upon a time was a long time ago.

"Please," I whispered, and he frowned, as if confused that
anything in this hellish place was still alive. "They'll come for us
soon. I've seen how they work."

He glanced from me to one of the empty beds and his jaw
tightened.

He knew.

The next time those faceless things in black came, they'd drag
me out, strap me to the newly emptied bed. Start their work,
whatever the purpose was.

I glanced down at the thin woman curled behind me in the
cage, burning up with fever. They'd do the same to her, she just
wouldn't last as long.

I waited. The giant knew what happened here. If that wasn't
enough to get him to save us, nothing I said would matter.

He glanced at the corners of the lab, at the shiny black half-
domes mounted in each vertex. The panels around them lit and
blinked during the experiments. I'd wondered if they were
cameras, but at the time it didn't matter.

The man reached for the door of the cage and frowned, his
eyes looking behind me to Loree's still body.

"You have to help us both. She needs me." She was my patient.
Which might sound ludicrous here, but it was all I had to hold on
to anymore.

With a twist of his hand the lock on the cage door crumpled.

I reached for Loree to pull her out with me and winced. Her
clammy skin was dull, and she no longer responded to my touch.

"Move." The word was a low rumble, and I flinched, eyes wide.

Our rescuer stood by the cage, waiting for me to get out of his way.

Come on, Nadira, you don't have any other choices. I stepped back and watched as he reached through the door and eased Loree out and into his arms with surprising gentleness.

He stood, bearing her weight on his left arm, her head and arms flung over his shoulder like a sleepy child, and headed toward the door.

"Wait, what about the others?"

I glanced back at six remaining patients. Patient wasn't the right word. Victims. Sacrifices to some angry god of pain.

He disappeared with Loree, and I knew he was right. There was nothing I could do for them now.

"I'll be back," I whispered, tears stinging my eyes. And then I followed the stranger into the dark corridor.

At first I couldn't find him in the dark hall, my eyes too used to the bright lights of the lab. I strained my ears, but heard nothing.

Fine. Left or right. Right?

Turning sharply, I kept my hand trailing against the right side wall of the corridor.

Instead of the cold metal plating I'd imagined, soft fabric ran under my fingers, interrupted in places. Any other time, I'd have stopped, curious to explore the mystery. Now I just wanted to put as much distance between me and the horror as possible.

My heartbeat pounded in my ears. Shouldn't I be able to see the man and Loree ahead of me by now?

Two, three more tentative steps, then a warm hand engulfed my upper arm.

"No. This way." He tugged me along and as we moved through the empty halls. Tiny lights flickered by our feet as we went and I began to make out some details of our surroundings.

Rich red fabric upholstered the walls, but it was ripped and stained, the pattern faded. I squinted at it as we passed, a distant memory tickled.

"Where are we?"

"Base."

Right then. Not long on conversation. As long as he could get us to safety, I didn't care.

Before long, a hatch blocked the corridor, lights flashing red and yellow around the seal.

"What are you doing?" I pulled back, but there was nowhere else to go. "There's no atmosphere beyond there!"

Every child raised on a station knew that pattern, every passenger on every ship throughout the Empire was taught it.

Hull breach. Unsurvivable.

He muttered something, then sat Loree on the deck, leaning against the wall. I rushed to her, but she was the same: burning hot, unresponsive.

"Why would you save us from the cage to bring us here?"

He grunted, massive arms bulging as he wrenched the wheel of the manual release.

Even as I flung myself over Loree, I knew it was pointless. There wasn't anything to hang onto, and after the cage, I wasn't strong enough anyway.

But the rush of vacuum didn't rip through the hall. Not a flutter.

Rolling off of Loree I sat, blinking. The man stood above us, and through the sliver of open hatch I could see a perfectly safe looking hallway, just like the one we'd been in.

"Coming?"

Click here to keep reading Freed!

NEED TO CATCH UP ON THE STAR BREED?

Don't miss a single one!

Given: Star Breed Book One

When a renegade thief and a genetically enhanced mercenary collide, space gets a whole lot hotter!

Thief Kara Shimsi has learned three lessons well - keep her head down, her fingers light, and her tithes to the syndicate paid on time.

But now a failed heist has earned her a death sentence - a one-way ticket to the toxic Waste outside the dome. Her only chance is a deal with the syndicate's most ruthless enforcer, a wolfish mountain of genetically-modified muscle named Davien.

The thought makes her body tingle with dread-or is it heat?

Mercenary Davien has one focus: do whatever is necessary to get the credits to get off this backwater mining colony and back into space. The last thing he wants is a smart-mouthed thief -

even if she does have the clue he needs to hunt down whoever attacked the floating lab he and his created brothers called home.

Caring is a liability. Desire is a commodity. And love could get you killed.

http://myBook.to/StarBreed1

Bonded: Star Breed Book Two

She doesn't need anyone. He's not going to let her go.

Eris Vance, salvager and loner, is happy with her life in the remote fringes of the Empire with just her AI for company. An abandoned ship could be the find of a lifetime, but it's not nearly as empty as she thinks. And the hulking man left behind kindles a heat she's never felt. But will he stay through the coming storm?

Connor is the perfect soldier - He's been made that way. Waking up to the destruction of the world he knew disturbs him almost as much as the gorgeous woman who found him. Her scent, her touch distracts him, and just this once, maybe he doesn't care.

The *Daedelus* is filled with secrets and the results of genetic experiments to breed the perfect soldier... and now that she's awakened him, the mystery of its destruction will hunt them both. Can the growing bond between them survive?

http://myBook.to/StarBreed2

Caged: Star Breed Book Three

No Past. No Trust. No Way Out.

Zayda Caiden relies on no one. An Imperial spy, her mission was betrayed - but she doesn't know the identity of the traitor.

And there's certainly no reason to trust the giant of a man

dumped at the prison clinic, even if he makes her burn with feelings she thought long buried.

Mack has no memory, no real name. Just dreams of fire and pain, and a set of coordinates to a section of unexplored space he refuses to reveal. There's no room in his mission for a woman with secrets of her own, but her scent fills his dreams.

When they have a chance at freedom, can they trust each other enough to escape? Or will their secrets overwhelm their passion?

http://myBook.to/Starbreed3

Freed: Star Breed Book Four

When solitude leads to the brink of madness, only the touch of a sexy, headstrong doctor can pull a dangerous warrior back from the edge...

Dr. Nadira Tannu's work at the small clinic on Orem station was a quiet practice, helping the people of the Fringe. But then she and one of her patients were abducted into a nightmare on a long lost star ship and nothing would ever be the same.

When a rugged survivor rescues them, can she turn his thirst for revenge into a plan for escape? And can she keep her heart safe from the heat in his eyes?

Vengeance against the faceless droids who destroyed his brothers is all that keeps Ronan alive. But he can't resist the pleading look in a pair of wide green eyes staring at him from a cage.

He'll keep her safe. Even if it's from himself.

http://myBook.to/Starbreed4

Craved: Star Breed Book Five

Compassion. Kindness. Caring.

Not really part of my skill set. But for her, I might have to learn.

Geir

I run advance reconnaissance, collecting intel the Pack needs to execute our operations.

In and out, hard and fast.

And I don't need help.

So when a gorgeous woman saves my life, I'm knocked more than a bit off my game.

That's all it is.

Not the shy smile I hunger to coax from her lips, not the sweet body she keeps hidden. Not the mysteries that haunt her eyes.

And certainly not the bewitching scent that stirs me in ways no mission ever has.

I crave her like nothing I've found before.

Even if she might be the enemy, I'll make her mine.

Valrea

He can't save me.

The secrets of the Compound are too tangled. The nightmares in my blood can never be erased.

But his touch sends me reeling, thirsting for what I can't have.

What harm could one night do?

http://myBook.to/Starbreed5

Snared: Star Breed Book Six

When the only woman Xander cared for was ripped from his arms, nothing else mattered.

Now she's back. Fragile and brave, beautiful and brilliant. Someone to protect, someone to fight for.

Except she doesn't remember him at all.

Her curves and captivating scent drive him mad, demanding he cares for her, possess her.

He'll keep his mate safe, even if the Empire burns to ash around them.

Loree Sarratt is tired of everyone treating her like an invalid. Her hacking skills could save the Empire - if she's not arrested first.

First puzzle to solve? An overprotective pillar of muscle who turns her legs to jelly when he's in the same room.

She can't lose focus. But the heat of his gaze sends her pulse racing. His touch steals her breath. Everything tempts her to surrender...

And forget the danger she's in.

http://myBook.to/Starbreed6

PLEASE DON'T FORGET TO LEAVE A REVIEW!

Readers rely on your opinions, and your review can help others decide on what books they read. Make sure your opinion is heard – http://myBook.to/StarBreed3

If you're interested in keeping up with future releases and opportunities for advance review copies, please join the newsletter! http://elinwynbooks.com/newsletter/

ABOUT THE AUTHOR

I love old movies – *To Catch a Thief, Notorious, All About Eve* — and anything with Katherine Hepburn in it. Clever, elegant people doing clever, elegant things.

I'm a hopeless romantic.

And I love science fiction and the promise of space.

So it makes perfect sense to me to try to merge all of those loves into a new science fiction world, where dashing heroes and lovely ladies have adventures, get into trouble, and find their true love in the stars!

ALSO BY ELIN WYN

The Empire's Fringe – Science Fiction Romance
The Empire's Fringe Bundle
All of the below stories, at a special price!
https://elinwynbooks.com/the-empires-fringe/
Staked

In the slums of space station Cilurnum 8, fiercely independent Anisha Cheng must decide how far she's willing to trust Kieran Matthias, the one man who she's ever allowed to break her heart. If she can't, she risks losing the Sapphire Star, her late father's bar and the only home she knows, to a crime syndicate in three days. But as Anisha and Kieran try to work together, the plans of the syndicate may break them apart forever.

Jewel of Empire

On the spaceliner Dynomius, reformed cat burglar Audrey Pilgram has three weeks to prove her innocence of a series of copycat crimes, or all the sins of her past will be laid at her door. But her quest to uncover the culprit is complicated when she sees the next target - tall, handsome Phillip Lapsys. Can she stop the theft of the jewel before he steals her heart?

Raven's Heart

Jayna wasn't looking for trouble. Her plan was to keep her head down, save her money, and get back into to med school. But when she overhears the plans for a bio-terrorism attack that could wipe out the population of her station, her world is turned upside down. Raven's Heart is a steamy science fiction romance complete novella with a happy ending, containing nebula hot scenes of passion.

Stolen

An alien artifact. Archaeologist Eliya Cafeal has spent her life in pursuit of this find - and nothing is going to get in her way. Certainly not a rogue and a scoundrel, even if he makes her blood catch fire. Captain Ruvon Taxal likes his life. Few close friends, a spot of petty smuggling or charter trips as needed. No restrictions, and nothing to tie him down. And if his newest passenger, a feisty archaeologist with storm grey eyes, has gotten under his skin, well, he'll learn to live without her when she leaves. But everything is changed when Eliya is stolen.

Claimed

In the remote mountains of a frontier planet, tinkerer and part-time inventor Paige Roth has her hands full protecting her claim against the goons of MagnorCo. With the help of her robots, she's doing pretty well, but the last thing she expects to fall into one of her traps is a handsome stranger trying to hike through the mountains for reasons of his own. He's handsome enough to make her forget where she put her toolkit, but can she trust him?

ALIEN WARRIOR ROMANCE

https://elinwynbooks.com/alien-romance/

Alien Mercenary's Desire: Alien Abduction Romance

Kordiss has spent his life on the fringe, not succumbing to his rages. But when he rescues feisty human Sharla from intergalactic sex traders, his defenses are breached by her trusting smile. And when she's stolen from his arms, nothing will stand in the way of getting her back.

This is a sexy, steamy stand-alone alien abduction short romance with a happy ending.

Bonded to the Alien: Gate Jumpers Saga Part 1

Captain Taryn Nephalia was, honestly, a little bored with her current mapping mission. But a freak accident sent her and her crew crashing towards an unknown planet. Captured by alien snake men, Taryn knows she's on her own to escape, rescue her crew, and get off that rock.

But she's not expecting help from a fellow prisoner - a hunky alpha alien warrior on mission of his own. And now his mission includes her.

Bonded to the Alien is the first in a linked series of steamy science fiction alien romance short stories about Captain Taryn and her crew.

Allied with the Alien: Gate Jumpers Saga Part 2

Stephine Willovitch isn't sure about trusting the Eiztar warriors. She's practical, logical, and not terribly fond of strangers. As far as she remembered, she'd just entered her pod moments ago. Torpor gas had kept her still for the past 36 hours. But apparently Captain Taryn had gotten them all involved with a bunch of rebels, and now they were on the run from some sort of alien snake men. Stephine would follow orders, but she couldn't be ordered to trust the man paired with her - Dojan Cholsad-. Tall, blond, stunningly handsome - and annoyingly friendly - she certainly wasn't going to put up with any of this bonding nonsense. But when Dojan is in danger, her heart isn't listening to her head.

Trapped with the Alien: Gate Jumpers Saga Part 3

Sherre Balinko, the navigator and youngest of Captain Taryn's crew, couldn't be more excited. She might be stranded on a hostile alien planet, but now they were allied with a whole new group of aliens! Her partner in the race to get the antitoxin back to the base is the tall, handsome Zaddik Wangari. But the grand adventure is over When the Tuvarians board the Eiztar mothership and Sherre and Zaddik must battle them alone...

Lost with the Alien: Gate Jumpers Saga Part 4

Jeline Montias, human pilot, isn't thrilled about being paired with Kogav Wangari of Zurole. He's flippant, grumpy and even though he's an engineer and not a pilot, reluctant to let her at the controls. Why should she care that he has eyes like gorgeous amethyst pools and a sweet smile?

They can't seem to stop arguing, even when they're dodging Tuvarian raiders in their mission to get a deadly poison back to the Eitzar lab for analysis. But when they're driven through a set of jump gates to a new sector, they'll have to work together to survive.

Science Fiction Adventure Romance

Join the men of the Garrison as they discover the secrets of Crucible...

Second Chance at the Stars:

As a gifted psychokinetic healer, Adena Thornwood's skills are in constant demand. She's built a solid reputation for her willingness to make sacrifices at any cost. But when she's betrayed by members of her own family, she may finally be broken. Regaining control will be near impossible with her heart in shambles.

Suppressing the rebellion on Crucible should have been just another mission for Commander Nic Vistuv and the men of his garrison unit. But lies and misinformation plague their mission from the beginning. Ghosts from the past haunt them, threatening his life and those of his brothers-in-arms.

The only way out of their predicament may lie in the form of a bribe, but this bribe is different. It's wrapped in the body of a young healer, whom is battle-scarred and broken by a deep betrayal. As secrets unravel and enemies draw nearer, Adena may be the key to understanding the truth of Crucible.

Can a wounded healer and an embittered soldier come to trust each other in time to forge a second chance for both?

http://elinwynbooks.com/my-books/